P9-EDE-107

# MAGNUM
# FAULT

# MAGNUM FAULT

## RABOO RODGERS

Houghton Mifflin Company
Boston

*Library of Congress Cataloging in Publication Data*

Rodgers, Raboo.
  Magnum fault.

  Summary: Jill and Cody solve a mystery that begins
with the disappearance of Jill's father, a geologist
for a gas company, after he has made a frightening
discovery, and the sudden drying-up of Cody's favorite
canoeing river.
  [1. Mystery and detective stories.   2. Gas industry—
Fiction.   3. West (U.S.)—Fiction]   I. Title.
PZ7.R6157Mag  1984        [Fic]        83-22798
ISBN 0-395-34558-8

Printed in the United States of America

Q  10  9  8  7  6  5  4  3

for Rebecca

*With special appreciation to physicist-biologist James E. Brazil and combat helicopter pilot Don R. Thompson, both of whom contributed essential technical assistance.*

# 1.

JILL WAS COMING FULLY AWAKE NOW. THE NIGHT SPEED was lifting the fog of sleep that shrouded her brain, and she was beginning to grasp the degree of urgency that had caused her father to shake her from a deep slumber only minutes earlier.

The sports car's engine screamed, and the gravel spewed by its tires into the undercarriage was a continuous, deafening roar. She bit her lip as her father threw the car into a controlled slide around the sharp angle of a hairpin curve, and then he rammed the throttle to the floor again, accelerating up the rocky mountain road.

She had to shout to make herself heard. "I don't understand! What is it? What's wrong?"

In the amber glow of the instrumentation, she saw her father shake his head, too preoccupied with his driving to answer her. But his actions told her something had to be terribly wrong, and she detected something in his expression that she had never seen there before — fear. Nathan Faraday was a man who had never feared anything, and seeing him afraid now made a tight, hard knot form deep inside her.

"Daddy! What is it? Tell me!"

The sports car crested the top of the mountain with such speed that it was airborne momentarily, its headlights cutting a swath through dark space, the road falling away beneath them.

Leaving her stomach hanging queasily, the car came down again, the suspension bottoming out hard as the wheels were slammed upward into the fender wells. The rear end lost traction, and they began to slide, this time toward the edge of the road and the two hundred feet of nothingness that terminated on rocks and boulders strewn along the bank of the Patawa River.

But her father was an expert. Machines were second nature to him. He made a minor correction, and the car straightened. They raced on, shooting down the side of the mountain and across the low-water bridge of Duck Creek and then up again toward the next crest, the car wagging and nearly overrunning itself under the heavy foot of its driver. The automobile took such punishment that Jill expected something to break at any moment.

"Daddy!" she shouted, pressing him. "What is it? Tell me before I go crazy!"

The road ran straight for a few hundred yards, and Nathan Faraday glanced at his daughter, his worried expression changing suddenly to one of tenderness and affection. He doted on his teenage daughter. Each was all the family the other had, and he had given her everything he could think of, as if he had deliberately wanted to spoil her. But

2

Jill hadn't needed very many things, and she had turned out to be sort of unspoilable.

It had been a mistake for her to have gone away to the private academy in St. Louis, she thought. It had been okay there, but she had missed her father. And she had missed having the opportunity to get to live in this rugged and beautiful area of the Ouachita Mountains, where Nathan Faraday had taken a job a year earlier as a senior geological engineer for Magnum Gas Company.

Jill had come home for summer vacation, and right away she had known that something was troubling her father. Now whatever was bothering him had suddenly escalated into something so serious that he had shaken her awake in the middle of the night without taking time to tell her why, and they were fleeing — apparently for their very lives.

"It's something I discovered in a routine aerial survey," he said over the din of the engine and spraying gravel. "Out there." He motioned toward the blackness, toward the hundreds of square miles that comprised the range of thick forests and mountains. "The way the fault line runs. I studied the data for a long time before I realized what it could mean." He shook his head again. "I should have known it would come to this. And I should have stopped you from coming back here, too. You would have been safe in St. Louis. I should have joined you there myself."

The road began to twist again, and he stopped talking to concentrate on his driving. Downshifting, he threw the car into another curve, into another controlled slide, and came out accelerating, spewing another fountain of gravel from the tires and winding the engine until the tachometer was redlined. Jill braced one hand against the dash and held on. The road leveled at the top of Thompson's Ridge, and as she leaned back in the deep bucket seat, something "out there" attracted her attention.

At first she thought it was a meteorite burning itself out in the starry sky above the ragged humps of the mountains. But then the point of light appeared to be rising, not falling.

Climbing in a graceful arc across the sky, it flickered initially, then grew in intensity. Within moments, it had become brilliantly white, a beam that slashed through the darkness like the edge of a knife.

It came closer, and then suddenly it slowed, almost stopping, hanging in the night like a giant lantern suspended by a huge, unseen hand. Jill felt a chill run the length of her spine as the light began to move again, gathering speed on a parallel course and racing ahead of them.

"What on earth!" she exclaimed. "What *is* that?"

She looked at her father and saw that as he held the car expertly to the road, he was watching the light, too. Streaking across the sky, the white sphere suddenly disappeared, winking out behind the bulk of the mountain ahead of them, and Nathan Faraday drove even faster.

Like the touch of icy fingers, an eerie feeling came over Jill. Her fear swelled, becoming a lump that she could feel above her pounding heart.

What was it? she wondered. *What was happening?*

The headlights illuminated a large rock in the middle of the road, and her father swerved, trying to avoid a collision, but they were moving too fast. Faraday centered the car over the rock, and it struck the undercarriage with a force that

4

sounded like an explosion, shearing away the car's muffler and tail pipe.

The car staggered, then regained its speed, popping and roaring so loudly that the added noise produced a distorting pain in Jill's ears. Slicing behind an outcrop on the final stretch toward the main highway, the road bent and angled downward. They were midway through the bend when night turned to day.

Rising suddenly from behind the outcrop, the light assumed a position above and in front of them and hung there like a white-hot sun, blinding them with its brilliance.

Her father stood on the brakes, and Jill screamed. She felt the car spinning out of control, rolling, striking, rebounding. Then she was free, separate from it, floating.

The last thought she had was that she had neglected to fasten her seat belt.

# 2.

RILEY HEARD IT FIRST. HE WOULD NOT HAVE PAID MUCH attention to it, because he had a general disinterest in the sounds of mechanical things, but he had previously made a connection between the appearance of this object and the level of excitement he sensed in his master, so his ears perked up in response to the first fluttering pulses.

Riley was Cody's Irish setter, a muscular, big-boned dog whose flowing red coat was so sleek that, when it was clean and brushed, it was almost possible to see a mirror image in it. Right now, however, it was plastered against his slablike shoulders, dripping. Until Cody had called him back into the canoe, he had been happily chasing fish in the shallows at the edge of a gravel bar. Sometimes a sunfish or bass would come into only a few inches of water to feed, and the first time Riley tried to catch one, he had succeeded.

He never caught another one, but he had come close a couple of times, and he had never forgotten the one he did catch. He tended to be obsessed with it, too, to become sort

6

of fish-chasing crazy, ramming his head under water to snap at anything from the size of a minnow on up. He would have preferred to do this without interruption, but most of the time Cody made him sit in the bow of the canoe, where his ninety pounds balanced everything out just right. That wasn't so bad, though. Riley also liked to sit and look and smell and hear.

Now Cody heard it, too — a smooth fluttering sound, a good sound. Gradually it became harder, with more of a staccato punch, and Cody wished he had a wider area of view. The trees were so thick and the terrain rose so quickly at the edges of the Patawa River that his line of sight was blocked toward the horizons. But a few moments later, it crossed overhead.

He craned his neck back to watch, to keep it in view as long as he could. It was a beauty, absolutely, he thought.

It was an ancient Stearman, an antique really, a collector's item, a true classic from the glorious era of biplanes. With staggered wings and open cockpits and a seven-cylinder radial engine, the marvelously restored blue-and-yellow aircraft took Cody's breath away. He tried to imagine what it would be like up there in the sky, in that plane. It had to be one of the finest feelings a person could have, he thought, and it was the only place he could think of where he might rather be for a little while than where he was right now.

He was able to see the plane for only a few seconds, but during that time it passed low enough that he could make out the helmets of the pilot and passenger and even see one of them turn and look down at him just before the Stearman banked and disappeared behind the treetops.

It was the fourth day Cody and Riley had been on the river and at least the sixth or seventh time they had seen the Stearman pass overhead. Somebody was cruising about and having fun up there, just as he and Riley were having fun down here.

Whoever owned the plane was probably keeping it at Kennethville, Cody decided. It always came from that general direction, and Kennethville's airport, although hardly more than a cow pasture, was the only one around.

"We're going to go have a look at that plane," he said to Riley, and Riley thumped his tail because he always thumped his tail when Cody said something to him. "Sometime next week we'll drive over. I just hope it'll still be there."

The idea of flight had always fascinated Cody. Voraciously, he read everything he could find about airplanes and flying, and deep inside he knew that somewhere in his future he would have an intimate relationship with an airplane. He was convinced that he was destined to fly.

Yet he had never even ridden in an airplane. In fact, he had seen only a few close up, and those had been very ordinary Cessnas or Pipers — nothing exotic and certainly nothing like the Stearman.

That was one of the problems with being from any of the small towns that lay isolated within the Ouachitas. It was so rural that the rest of civilization, with all of its sophisticated technologies, seemed another culture away. The only real change to come to the area in recent years was the introduction of satellite-receiving stations, so that people were now plugged in, via television, to both coasts and could readily see what was going on in the rest of the world.

But for Cody there were advantages in living here, too, the chief one being the Ouachita Mountains' forest and waterways, especially the Patawa. Cody loved this river and the country that surrounded it. It did something to him. It made him happy. It made him feel good. Whenever he could, he loaded his canoe with Riley and a minimum of gear and took the longest float for which there was time available.

From its headwaters near Sumlin to its junction with the larger Ouachita River at Baxter, the Patawa River twisted, turned, churned, and fell for almost two hundred miles. In trips that lasted from only a few days to more than two weeks, Cody had paddled all of that distance — and several times over. Two summers earlier, he had gone the entire route in a single run. For seventeen days, he had paddled the river, and for sixteen nights he had camped along its banks. He had been with Joe Tiotec then, and that had made it the best trip of all.

So flying may have been in his dreams, but the Patawa River was in Cody's heart. He knew that events would take him away from here one day — college was already close at hand — but until that time came, he was in no hurry to leave this magnificent country, not even to chase the sky.

The image of the Stearman fading in his mind, Cody returned his attention to the Patawa. He never got used to the way this river and the mountains that hugged it looked. He could never take them for granted. The banks and mountains were green and lush with an extravagance of native hardwoods, as thick as a tropical rain forest. Through this greenery sluiced the clear water of the Patawa. It poured between rocks into quiet pools, fell over low, stepped falls, turned frothing and white on narrow rapids, and shoaled across escarpments and gravel bars.

The Patawa abounded with fish and supported a rich variety of wildlife. Beaver, otter, whitetail deer, raccoon, muskrat, kingfishers, and even the bald eagle were a few examples among many, many more that Cody regularly saw in the immediate environs of the river. Every minute he was here was a time of learning and pleasure for him. He loved the Patawa, and he loved the forests and mountains surrounding it.

Sometimes he thought he loved it here almost as much as Joe Tiotec did.

A school of shad flashed beneath the bow, and Riley stood up suddenly to watch, rocking the canoe so that Cody had to make a quick, saving move with the paddle.

"Sit!" he ordered. "You've fooled with enough fish for one day."

Riley sat, but he hadn't fooled with enough fish.

Cody drew his paddle through the water again, coaxing the canoe ahead so he wouldn't fall too far behind schedule. There was something odd about having to hurry the canoe along this part of the river, he thought. There was usually more current than this. In fact, for the past half hour or so, he seemed to have had to put out significantly more effort with the paddle than he was used to. Maybe he was just getting tired.

But a few minutes later, he realized the extra effort required had nothing to do with his physical condition. Against the smooth face of a boulder at the river's edge, the watermark showed that the river had fallen as much as eight inches, and it had done it so quickly that Cody had not even been aware it was happening!

Puzzled, Cody backpaddled. The canoe easily went dead in the failing current, and as he stared at the watermark on the boulder, he actually saw the river fall another two to three inches!

Cody got a strange, creepy feeling. This made no sense at all. The spring rains had been regular and even, and the Patawa River drained a large area of country, accumulating water from many small sources. This time of the year, with no extremes of weather, its flow was ample and steady. But as he sat there wondering about it, the river fell even more. In a matter of only minutes, it had dropped by more than a foot!

Confused, Cody looked upstream. The last rapids he had come through had been reduced to little more than a trickle. In several places, they had run white. Now they hardly ran at all, and as he continued to watch, they came to a virtual halt.

For a moment, he wondered if he could be imagining this. But it was actually happening. The river had stopped flowing. Water from the pool where he was sitting in his canoe barely leaked through the rocks into the next pool below it. Fish had become trapped in shallows that were cut off from the main part of the river. A loggerhead turtle ambled for deeper water, because his resting place was now exposed.

For a long time Cody just sat, letting the morning breeze push the canoe in a lazy drift across the dead calm surface of the pool. He could not think of anything to explain what had happened, and not having an explanation was almost frightening.

11

Finally, there was nothing to do but get going again. The river may have stopped, but he couldn't. He paddled the length of the pool, then got out and began dragging the canoe over the rocks into the next pool, a process he would have to repeat over and over again. Today was to be the last day of his float trip — he anticipated reaching his take-out point early in the afternoon — but if he had to haul the canoe most of the way like this, it was going to be one of the longest days of his life.

Riley kept wanting to go after the fish. They would be easy pickings now, but Cody made him stay close to the canoe. He didn't know why he did that, but he felt uneasy about what had happened to the river, and having Riley beside him somehow helped.

He had been paddling and dragging the canoe, mostly dragging it, for more than an hour when a faint current began to stir around his feet. Then he heard a trickling noise, which gradually grew louder as water began to pour through the rocks. Minutes later, the current was aiding him, pushing the canoe as he pulled with the bow line.

Within another hour, the river was back to normal, sweeping them downstream at the familiar clip. Cody thought about it and thought about it. It was the strangest thing he had ever experienced. It was crazy. The entire river had stopped flowing, and then it had started up again.

Cody shook his head in total, absolute, confusion. "We'll ask Joe about it," he said. "If anybody has an explanation, it'll be Joe."

Riley thumped his tail.

# 3.

HER FIRST AWARENESS WAS OF BIRDS SQUAWKING. THERE was an altercation nearby between a pair of mockingbirds and a blue jay. She heard the flutter and beat of wings, but when she opened her eyes, she saw only a shadowed movement of the birds. There were things around her, green things, blocking her view.

With a sudden start, Jill tried to sit up, but whatever was supporting her sagged and canceled her effort, keeping her on her back, almost as if she were lying in a hammock.

In a flash, it came back to her. The racing car. The light. Her father.

"Daddy!"

She reached out and clutched a handful of the green things and saw that they were honeysuckle vines, a thick tangle of them. Pulling herself over to her side, she realized that in being thrown clear of the wreck, she had landed in one of the immense growths of honeysuckle that covered much of the roadside. She started to move again, to crawl out of the honeysuckle, but was stopped by a throbbing pain in her head.

Reaching up, she flaked dried blood from her forehead. From near her hairline, her fingers came back red and sticky with congealing blood. She had been knocked out long enough for the cut to have stopped bleeding on its own.

Struggling, she fought her way out of the vines and leaves and stood up. It was morning — and late in the morning. The sun was well into the sky. She had been unconscious for hours!

Stumbling and holding one hand to her aching head, she ran along the gravel shoulder. She remembered that she had been thrown out when the car first began to flip out of the curve, and she reasoned it should have left the road altogether about halfway or two thirds through the curve, after they were blinded by the light. Reaching that point, she looked down the slope, away from the roadbed.

"Daddy!" She cried out for him in anticipation of seeing the crumpled car and finding him injured — or worse. But what she saw made her stand there in disbelief. There was nothing — no mangled automobile, and no sign of her father. There was only open hillside, where the eastern part of the Ouachitas graduated to an isolated valley and the small town of Oak Flats. The hill where she stood sloped gently to a green pasture below it, and nowhere was there any sign of a wreck!

She ran back the way she had come, searching the hillside close to where she had disentangled herself from the honeysuckle. She went all the way back to the outcrop, where the light had suddenly appeared, causing them to wreck. She searched the side there, and still there was no sign of her father's car.

In the middle of the road, she looked for skid marks. But if they were there, they weren't readily apparent among the ruts and loose gravel, and there were a dozen or more tire tracks and marks on the shoulder, where people habitually swung too wide in going around the curve. Any of them could have been construed as evidence of an accident — except that apparently there hadn't been an accident.

But there *was* an accident, she thought, and her mind went back over it again. She remembered the strange, blinding light, the car beginning to roll, the feeling of being thrown through the air.

She retraced her steps along the shoulder, searching again, and now she began to feel panicked. Her head throbbed, and all she could think of was that her father was lying injured, possibly dead, and she couldn't even find him.

The sound of an automobile engine snatched her attention, and, yelling and waving her arms, she ran into the middle of the road. A pickup truck carrying an elderly farm couple slowed to a stop.

"Oh, my goodness, honey!" the woman said from the passenger window. "What awful thing has happened to you?"

Frantic, Jill explained. "My father and I had a wreck! I was thrown out! I can't find him!"

The old man came out of the truck with surprising speed. "Show me where!"

"Harold, the poor girl's hurt," the woman said. "She can't —"

But Jill was already running, pointing. "The car turned

over right about there! It should have gone over the hill. I was thrown into those vines!"

The spry old man ran to the side of the road and stopped. He looked, and then he looked again. Like Jill, he went along the shoulder, looking down the slope.

"Where could he have gone?" she asked helplessly.

The farmer shook his head. "I don't know, but I sure don't see no car. Are you for certain it turned over?"

"Yes," she said, nodding.

"How did it happen?"

"We — we were blinded by a light. My father couldn't —"

"A light?" The farmer looked surprised. "It happened at night?"

"Yes," she replied. "It was dark — after midnight."

"That's been a long time."

She nodded. "I was unconscious until a few minutes ago."

The farmer regarded her thoughtfully and with concern. "They might of already got your daddy, sugar. If you was thrown into them vines, they mightn't of seen you. And if your daddy was hurt and couldn't tell 'em, then they wouldn't have no way of knowin' you was in the car, too. The ambulance might of took him, and then the sheriff would of sent for a wrecker to get the car. And they mightn't have never saw you."

Of course! Jill thought. That made sense. She would have realized that herself if she hadn't been frantic and dazed. Her father had been hurt and couldn't talk. But maybe he was only knocked out, as she had been. Oh please! she thought. Don't let him be dead!

"We need to get you to a doctor," the farmer said. "We'll

16

take you to the clinic in Oak Flats. That's probably where they would of carried your father, too."

It was hardly more than a ten-minute drive to Oak Flats, but that was more than long enough for Jill to realize she didn't feel so good. Not only did her head hurt, but she also had other aches and pains and one entire side of her body felt bruised.

She was grateful for the kind attention of the farmer's wife, who gently wiped the dirt from Jill's face with a handkerchief and said, "There, there, honey, you'll be all right now. You'll find your daddy, and everything will be fine. You just try to be calm until we can get a doctor to have a look at you."

But she couldn't stop worrying about her father, and at the clinic the two nurses on duty had to restrain her to make her lie down so she could be wheeled inside.

"My father was in the accident, too," Jill said, looking at the faces above her as she was rolled through a doorway. "Was he brought here?"

One of the nurses smiled at her. "You're the first emergency for us in three days, darling. If your father was hurt, he may have been taken to Kennethville. They have a hospital up there."

"I've got to find out!" she said pleadingly. "I've got to know!"

The farmer's wife was beside her, holding her hand. "Don't you worry, honey. I'll have Harold call the sheriff. He'll know what's happened to your daddy."

A middle-aged doctor with a kind smile appeared in the emergency room. He bent over her and ordered one nurse to remove her torn clothing while he probed around the cut on her head and the other nurse took her blood pressure and pulse.

The doctor looked studiously into Jill's eyes with a lighted instrument. He told her to watch his hand as he moved it across in front of her face. Then he had her bring her fingers together, touching the tip of her nose.

"Do you feel injured anywhere other than your head?" he asked.

"My side hurts," she said.

He touched her ribs and pressed. "Here?"

She caught her breath. "Yes!"

"Hmmm." He pressed some more, making her wince with pain. "You've got a nice bruise there, young lady, and a few scratches elsewhere, but nothing's broken. I'm going to have to take some stitches in your head, but it's a clean cut, so there won't be much of a scar." He looked down at her and smiled. "Besides, as pretty as you are, it would take a dozen scars before any of the other girls would even have a chance."

"Doctor, do you think my father could have been taken to the hospital at Kennethville?"

"Well, I haven't heard anything, but then those folks up at Kennethville don't always tell me every time they have a new admission."

A few minutes later, after he had injected Novocain around the cut and was pulling tight the first stitches, he said, "Your vital signs look good, young lady. There doesn't appear to be anything wrong with you that a few days of taking it easy won't cure. However, the fact that you were knocked out indicates that your brain took a pretty good jolt. You may have received a little concussion, certainly a contusion. To be on the safe side, I want you to promise me that you'll rest for the next three or four days."

"After I find out what happened to my father," she said, as the sheriff entered the room.

The tall, lanky sheriff nodded at the doctor. From where Jill was lying with her head turned, she could see a young deputy stopping a few feet behind him and the farmer and his wife hovering in the doorway.

"There's been no report of any accidents in the county within the last twenty-four hours, miss," the sheriff said to Jill, "and the ambulance company hasn't transported anyone to Kennethville. Can you tell me what happened?"

As quickly as she could, Jill told him the story, describing how the light had cut across in front of them, then come up suddenly from behind the outcrop and blinded them, causing her father to lose control of the car. The sheriff looked puzzled about the light and pressed her for details. All she could tell him was what she had seen — that it had moved at different speeds across the sky, until finally it had appeared in front of them.

"Could it have been an airplane?" he asked.

"No. It moved too erratically."

"What then?"

"I — I don't know," she said. "All I know is that my father seemed to be trying to get away from it and it caused us to wreck."

"Then your father could still be out there."

"But we couldn't find him!" she said, feeling her panic rise again. "We looked!"

19

"Well, I better go take another look," the sheriff said, turning to the farmer who had helped her. "The earth just doesn't swallow up whole cars. Harold, will you show Frank and me where you found her?"

"I will, Sheriff," the farmer replied. "But there ain't nothing there."

"We'll look anyway," the sheriff said. "We can't take any chances that a man is lyin' out there hurt."

# 4.

SHE WAITED, AND THE WAITING WAS UNBEARABLE. THEY left her in the emergency room, and she lay on her back looking up at the silver reflector of the big overhead light. The nurses wandered in and out, always smiling comfortingly, and Mrs. Haskins, the farmer's wife, came to stand by her and pat her arm reassuringly.

Jill was thankful that these people were here, but she could not quell the terror she felt about her father. She tried desperately to be optimistic, but the deep sense of foreboding would not leave her.

Again and again, she replayed the events in her head. Her father had shaken her awake, hardly giving her enough time to put on her shoes as he hurried her to the car. Then they were driving, and he was trying to tell her about something he had discovered "out there."

The light had come from out of the darkness, from "out there." Then it had gone ahead of them, disappearing before coming up as bright as the sun from behind the outcrop. What was it?

She knew it wasn't an airplane. She was certain about that. Her father was an expert pilot, and he had begun teaching her to fly when she was still a child. She had made her first unassisted landing when she was only eleven years old. At school in St. Louis the past year, she had turned seventeen and gotten her private pilot's license — much to the enjoyment of her friends, whom she often took aloft with her. So she knew more than enough about planes to be absolutely sure that the light in the night sky had not come from one.

She was still trying to determine what it could have been, when the sheriff returned. She looked up expectantly, but he shook his head.

"We didn't find anything, miss. Not your father or the car, either one. There's just not anything there."

"Then what could have happened?" she asked, sinking into a deeper feeling of despair.

"I'm sure we'd all like to know the answer to that. Maybe you better tell me again how you happened to have the accident."

Exasperated, Jill went over it again, telling him everything she remembered. He pressed her for greater detail about the strange light, but there was nothing she could say to explain it.

The sheriff looked at his deputy, and the deputy shrugged. They both seemed as mystified as she was.

"Your father is Nathan Faraday, and he works for Magnum Gas," the sheriff said, looking at notes he had taken.

"Yes. He's a geologist-engineer."

"Both of those?"

"Yes."

"And you live at Center Ridge?"

"In the country outside of there," she said. "About five miles from town."

"Is there anyone over there we can contact?"

Jill thought a moment. "We just moved to Center Ridge last year. I was only there for the summer before I went to school in St. Louis. I — I didn't get to know very many people."

The sheriff flipped his note pad over and looked up at her. "Well, I'll do some calling around."

"What good will that do?" she asked.

He shook his head. "I don't really know, but it's the only thing I can think of to do right now. This all seems a little strange to me."

"Yes, I agree. It's more than strange," she said.

The sheriff left to use the office phone, and Jill tried to resign herself again to waiting, but this time she didn't even know what she was waiting for. She quickly grew tired of lying there, and when the doctor came in, she got permission to sit up.

She drew the sheet around her and felt better in an upright position. Her perspective had suffered lying on her back. Her head still hurt, but the Novocain dulled the pain. Her ribs only hurt when she breathed.

The nurse took her blood pressure again, and the doctor looked into her eyes once more, telling her reassuringly, "All I see in there is a lot of bright blue prettiness."

23

As the doctor was putting away his instrument, the deputy appeared at the door and said that the sheriff wanted to see him in the clinic's office.

The doctor was gone for what seemed a long time to Jill, and when he finally returned, the sheriff was with him. Jill noticed a change in their expressions, and she interpreted that as information about her father. She was right.

"Good news," the sheriff said, smiling. "We located your father, and he's all right."

Jill experienced a sudden, enormous feeling of relief. "Oh thank goodness! Where is he? What happened to him?"

The sheriff exchanged glances with the doctor, then looked back at Jill. "Well, nothing really happened to him, miss. He's at work."

"At work?"

"Yes, he's out in the field." The sheriff looked at his note pad. "Doing studies of some kind. Uh, size, size —"

"Seismological," Jill said. "But that can't be! He was with me!"

The sheriff looked at the doctor, and the doctor said, "Apparently not. You see, he's been out in the field for the past two days."

"Did you talk to my father?"

"Yes, we did," the sheriff replied. "We called Magnum Gas, and their main office patched us through to him by radio."

"But that's crazy!" she said. "He was with me! We had a wreck! We —" She put her hands to her head. It was beginning to throb.

The sheriff and the doctor exchanged looks again, and the

24

doctor said, "Remember what I said about your brain being jolted pretty good? It's not uncommon at all for a person's memory to get scrambled somewhat in a case like this. It's not anything to worry about, Jill, but it is another indication that you need to take things real easy for a while. Okay?"

"No!" she countered, shaking her head and making it hurt more. "I remember perfectly! Right up until the very instant of the wreck!"

"Your father also explained that you just returned from St. Louis a few days ago," the doctor said. "A sudden change of surroundings like that, coupled with a blow to the head, could very likely confuse anybody's mind. It may come back to you all of a sudden." He smiled at her again and snapped his fingers for emphasis. "Just like that!"

"Then how did I end up beside the road?" she asked.

"That will probably come back to you also."

"Maybe you hitchhiked — with the wrong people," the sheriff suggested.

"I don't hitchhike."

"Whatever it is, I'm sure there's a logical explanation for it," the doctor said, "and in time we'll find it out. The important thing is for you not to get upset about it."

"I want to see my father," she said, very much upset about it.

"Yes, of course," the doctor replied. "Your father's company is hurrying to bring him in as soon as possible. In the meantime, they're sending a car to take you to Green Meadows. Are you familiar with Green Meadows?"

Green Meadows was a private hospital in one of the wooded valleys between Center Ridge and Oak Flats. She didn't know much about it, but she had driven past it a couple of times the previous summer. It had iron gates and a vast lawn that looked like rolling green velvet. "It looks expensive," she said.

The doctor laughed good-naturedly. "It is! But you're fortunate. Your father works for a company that has an excellent health plan for its employees and their dependents. So you don't have to worry about the expense. Green Meadows has the best facilities around — much better than those at the Kennethville hospital or what we have here in our clinic."

"I feel fine," she lied. "I don't need to go to a hospital."

"Your father thinks it would be a good idea," the doctor replied. "He'd rather you not be left alone, and I agree with him. I'm going to order you to rest anyway, so you may as well do it there, hadn't you?"

"I — I don't know," she mumbled, feeling suddenly very weak. "I just want to see my father."

"He'll see you at Green Meadows — as soon as he comes in," the doctor said with another reassuring smile. "And by then, your memory may have straightened itself out completely."

Jill lay down again and wondered how she could possibly be so wrong about something that seemed so clear. And how could her father have been in the field doing seismological testing for two days when she had been with him just yesterday? She could even remember what they had had for lunch.

But suddenly she did feel confused. It was all like some kind of terrible nightmare, where everything was horrible and nothing made sense. As the Novocain began to wear off, the pain in her head became more sharp, making it increasingly difficult for her to organize her thoughts. The more she tried, the more confusing everything became.

Within an hour, another nurse entered the emergency room. This nurse was dressed differently from the others, and Jill knew immediately that she did not work at the clinic.

"I'm Miss Edwards, Jill," the new nurse said in a friendly, professional way, "from Green Meadows." She handed her a package. "I brought this for you to put on. I think it will be more comfortable than the sheet."

It was a white gown, not the kind that was open down the back, but it was still a very institutional garment. Jill left the clinic wearing it and her sneakers. The nurse carried her torn clothes in a paper sack. Outside, a long dark limousine with a driver waited. The nurse noticed her surprise and smiled.

"Your father gave instructions that we are to take very special care of his daughter."

Sinking deeply into the plush upholstery in the back seat of the limousine, which seemed to float above the surface of the road, Jill felt an even greater loss of reality. The darkly tinted windows and the pain in her head altered her perception so that the world outside was like the shadowy background of a dream. She hardly noticed when they passed through the big iron gates onto the winding, shrub-and-tree-lined drive to the hospital.

An orderly with a wheelchair met the limousine, and although Jill felt capable of walking, the nurse insisted that she be wheeled inside.

"Rules," she said with a smile.

Everybody seemed to smile, Jill thought.

The hospital hardly resembled a hospital at all. The inte-

27

rior gave more of an impression of a quaint, and expensive, country inn. The furnishings were lavish. On the walls were tapestries and paintings, all conveying a sense of serenity. The orderly wheeled her down the hall and turned into a room near one end, leaving her with the nurse.

The room was like no other hospital room Jill had ever seen, either. It was homey and comfortable, with carpet so thick she could feel its cushiony softness through her shoes. There were stuffed chairs and a desk, a television and a big noninstitutional bed. In addition, there was a large picture window with an overview of the immaculate grounds and the woods beyond.

Nurse Edwards looked at her and smiled. "Don't you think it's lovely?"

"Yes," Jill admitted, "it is."

"Well now," the nurse continued, showing her the adjoining, richly tiled bathroom. "Your instructions are to rest, and that's easy to do here. I'm sure you'll find things pleasant and quiet."

"Yeah, it sure looks quiet all right," Jill said.

The nurse patted her reassuringly on the shoulder and backed out of the door. She smiled patiently. "Now don't you worry about a thing. Our entire staff is here to help you. Your only responsibility is to rest."

The door swung to, clicking softly behind the nurse. Jill reached for the handle, but the heavy door had locked automatically on being closed, and she saw there was no way to open it from the inside.

Her head was pounding, but she made another round of

the room, and now she began to realize how secure everything was. The place was built like a fortress.

At the window, she noticed the glass. It was thick and set in a molded steel frame. A sledgehammer would have had a hard time breaking it out.

Jill sat down on the bed and tried again to think. Everyone had told her not to worry, that everything was all right.

But everything wasn't all right, and she *knew* it wasn't.

# 5.

JOE TIOTEC WAS A DYING MAN. HIS EYES WERE MILKY WITH cataracts, and his steps were labored and painful. His body was rapidly running out of time, and when his life ended, so too would the last blood link to an extinct Indian culture be lost. Joe Tiotec was one-quarter Patawa Indian. After him, there were no others.

"It might not have been so noticeable this far downriver," Cody told him. "You still would have gotten water from Duck Creek. But I was above there. And the river stopped completely. Then an hour or two later, it started up again — just as if nothing had ever happened."

Cody watched Joe Tiotec carefully. In recent months, the old man seemed to have turned more and more inward, and sometimes Cody was not sure of getting through to him. But this time Joe was obviously listening.

"Yes," he said. "For an hour and forty minutes, the sustaining force of the Patawa did not exist. I, too, felt its life diminish, Cody."

30

Cody watched Joe Tiotec standing unsteadily at the edge of the river, while Riley waded in the shallows, looking for fish. For a moment, Cody again had that strange feeling that the weathered, aged man could actually communicate with the tumbling Patawa, as if they were both a part of the same entity.

"Why do you think it happened, Joe?" he asked cautiously.

Joe Tiotec turned slowly and looked at him. His eyes were so cloudy that Cody guessed he was hardly more than a blur to Joe.

"Perhaps the eagle swooped for a drink, and his thirst was extraordinary." It was meant as a joke, but Joe said it without humor.

"A million eagles couldn't have been that thirsty, Joe."

Joe Tiotec shook his head, and the feebleness with which he did it made Cody hurt inside. "What am I?" he asked.

Cody was a little confused by the question. "An anthropologist?"

"And a Patawa," the old man replied. "That fourth of me dominates the remaining three fourths of me, so that I become neither man nor anthropologist. I am the son of my mother, the grandson of her father, the great-grandson of his father and mother."

"You're talking about the beliefs of your ancestors," Cody said.

"Am I?" Joe Tiotec asked. "Can I not be speaking instead of the beliefs of an anthropologist?"

"Religion to an anthropologist is important primarily as evidence to help determine distribution, origin, and cultural classifications of people. You told me that yourself, Joe."

31

The lines in Joe Tiotec's face rearranged themselves into a wry smile that only Cody would have recognized. "Did I?" he asked, and there was a trace of amusement in the trembling of his voice this time. "Did I ever say such a thing?"

"Yes," Cody replied, "and a lot more things just like it."

Joe Tiotec's amusement increased. "Do you mean that I have been an advocate of scientific methods?"

"You know that you have," Cody said.

"That is to say, then, that there is an explanation for every happening?"

"Yes," Cody replied, detecting a spark in Joe Tiotec that he had not seen for months. "For everything there is a cause."

"And you believed me?"

"Yes," Cody said.

Joe Tiotec chuckled. "You are a good student, my young friend. Your senses are keen and your mind alert. You have learned well. But I caution you not to pursue logic as a zealot, for to be zealous is in itself an illogical act."

"I'm not sure I understand what you mean," Cody said.

Joe Tiotec turned toward the river and gestured to the water with one gnarled hand. "I mean that logic performs best for him who is receptive to all possibilities." He frowned now, the frown reflecting his physical pain. "When the Patawa's life was choked from it for an hour and forty minutes, the anthropologist would consider nothing beyond the unusualness of its occurrence. But the Indian, the lifeblood of the Patawa tribe, considered it an omen, an ill portent for the generations of his people and the sanctity of their Unity of One."

Cody listened, trying to be sure what Joe Tiotec meant. As the old man's health degenerated, he seemed to speak more and more in riddles, become more abstract — and less scientific — in his thought.

"What could cause the river to stop, Joe?"

Age had sagged the flesh on his face, and Joe Tiotec's cheekbones had become more prominent, altering the appearance of his features. Looking at him, Cody thought how alien he had finally become to the rest of society. But then he had never had much in common with other people that Cody knew.

"I do not know," he said in reply to Cody's question. "The scientist is limited in his endeavors this time by the passage of so many years. Only when his spirit is free can he reach out to the limits of knowledge."

More abstraction, Cody thought as he aided the old man along the river path back up to his cabin. Joe Tiotec sat down wearily in the wicker chair on the porch, and Riley curled up beside him while Cody went inside to bring him a glass of water.

The cabin was virtually empty now. Gone were the typewriter and stacks of books, all of his research papers and most of his furniture. Joe Tiotec had divested himself of nearly everything. It was another sign of the change that was coming over him in this final period of his life.

On the porch, Riley was resting his big head on Joe Tiotec's knee and looking up at him with worshipful eyes, while the old man's arthritic fingers gently caressed the base of the setter's ears. Cody gave Joe Tiotec the water, which he drank in small, slow swallows, and he asked if there was anything else he could do. He wanted to do more than Joe would allow.

He would have done anything that Joe asked, but Joe didn't ask, and Cody knew that was his cue to go, because Joe Tiotec did want something.

He wanted to be alone — alone to continue with the complexities of his final thoughts, carrying his powerful mind into a region that Cody could only respect without fully understanding. Joe Tiotec had taught Cody to look at life through the objective eyes of the scientist, yet still marvel at a world of wonder and beauty. It had been something they could share.

But now Joe Tiotec was facing something else, and the great difference in their ages made it something he had to face alone. For comfort, he seemed to have turned to the religion of his ancestors.

It was a beautiful belief, Cody thought. The Patawa Indians had considered themselves as one with their environment, not separate from it. It was why they had held the mountains and the river and the forests themselves to be sacred. At death, their spirits returned to the air and rock and earth and water that had temporarily given them the form of mortal man. This was what Joe Tiotec meant by the Patawas' Unity of One. It was the very basis of their philosophy and religion and had been the foundation of their culture.

Cody called Riley and turned to go, but Joe Tiotec stopped him.

"Cody," he said, his voice commanding little of the strength it had possessed only a few weeks earlier, "you must know this, my friend: If this were an earlier time, or there were not now laws of man to intervene, I would name you the bearer of my spirit."

Cody didn't know what to say. There wasn't anything he could say. The lump was so thick in his throat that he would have choked if he had tried to speak. But words weren't necessary. Joe Tiotec knew how he felt, and he motioned him on, almost urgently.

With Riley scouting the ivy along the path, Cody walked up the bank to where he had left his truck. A few minutes later he drove onto the high bridge a hundred yards downstream and then stopped the truck right in the middle of it. Absently, he placed one hand on the back of Riley's neck and looked upriver.

From here he could see Joe Tiotec's cabin nestled in the shade of hardwoods just above the high-water mark, and he could also make out Joe himself, sitting immobile on the front porch.

Joe had been born in that cabin, and he had grown up listening to the stories his mother told about the Patawas, an obscure, little-known Indian tribe that had existed for hundreds of years in the hills surrounding the Patawa River. Joe Tiotec had excelled in public school, and as a young man, he had gone away to an eastern university, where he earned graduate degrees in anthropology.

Unlike the majority of eager young anthropologists, he had shown only small enthusiasm for the great rush of research that at the time was probing the beginnings of mankind on the Horn of Africa. Instead, Joe Tiotec elected to return to the Ouachita Mountains and pursue a lifelong study of his own ancestors, the tribe of Indians called the Patawas.

Now his work was done. His final papers were safely in the archives at the state capital, and the land of the Patawas, largely through his own letter-writing efforts, had been declared inviolate as a natural preservation by the state legislature.

Cody's vision blurred, and he wiped away the tears that were beginning to pool in his eyes. In the ancient way of the Patawas, a person closest to the deceased was made bearer of his spirit. This was a great honor. The bearer's job was to take the body into the forest and bury it in an unmarked grave. The Patawas built no monuments to the dead, believing instead in the Unity of One. The spirit of the individual returned to the environment.

To Cody it seemed unfair that the last Patawa would not be allowed the ritual of his ancestors, but as Joe Tiotec had said, there were laws now, and one person was no longer permitted to take another person's body into the woods and bury him. The thought itself would have to suffice.

Cody saw a car coming in his side-view mirror. Putting the truck in gear, he started up again and drove on across the bridge toward town.

"It's not going to be the same without Joe," he said to Riley, and Riley thumped his tail.

# 6.

JILL'S HEART WAS RACING, BOOMING IN HER EARS. SHE gathered the hospital gown up around her waist so she wouldn't trip over the thing, and then she ran, skirting the outside perimeter of light from the corner floodlamp and reaching the blackness beneath the first big oak tree. She paused there, looking past the next patch of moonlight to the long shadow of the woods.

The corner of the fence was a little more to the right, she thought.

Glancing briefly in the direction of the hospital, she took another gather in the gown and ran again, sprinting through the silver moonlight and continuing on, her shoes wet and slippery on the dew-laden grass. By accident or intuition, she stopped at the last possible moment. She was not where she thought she was, and in another two steps she would have run face-first into the fence.

One hand on the chain-link wire, she followed the fence

to the corner, where she jammed her toes into the squares and began climbing. The gown was a terrible nuisance, and when she reached the three strands of barbwire at the top of the eight-foot fence, it became a hazard to her life.

Each time she tried to work her way over the razor-sharp strands, the gown defeated her, wrapping around or impaling itself on the barbs. She tried to squeeze between the first and second strands, but the gown stopped her the instant she attempted to put one leg through.

Finally she gathered the gown up in front and held it tucked beneath her chin. She called on her sense of balance now to get her over the top. One hand holding to the steel rod that supported the wire at the corner, she began stepping upward from one strand to the next. When she reached the topmost strand, she was bent over, balancing there. The only thing she could do was jump.

She shoved off with her feet, out into the black void, but she didn't jump far enough away from the fence. In the back, the gown still trailed below her waist, and as she fell, the barbwire snagged the hem.

For an instant, she thought she was going to be hung up by her armpits. Her momentum was brought up abruptly, in a series of hard jerks, and she swung backward, toward the fence. Then, with a loud tearing sound, the fabric yielded to her weight, and she fell the rest of the way, leaving part of the gown dangling like a banner from the top of the fence.

Surprised by the mildness of the impact with the ground, she gathered herself together and caught her breath. Then, stripping away the ragged pieces of gown and holding the remainder close around her, she began angling through the woods so she would not reach the main road until she was well away from Green Meadows Hospital.

The woods were so dark she could hardly see, and at every step sawbriar and vines impeded her movement. The forest floor, soft with mulch and decaying vegetation, also provided impediments. She stepped into a hole up to her knee, falling and sending some kind of squeaking animal scrambling wildly out of her way. This part of the country supported a variety of snakes, including copperheads, water moccasins, and rattlesnakes, and she tried not to think about what would happen if she stumbled across one in the dark.

She realized now that she had handled things badly during the past week, when she had been kept at the hospital. She should have escaped from there immediately, but in the beginning she had become so outraged, when they refused to let her leave, that she had been unable to keep from venting her anger and frustration at them. And the angrier she became at them and the more she insisted that she and her father had been in a wreck, the more closely they watched her.

Finally, she had gotten smart. She began cooperating with them, even smiling. (They seemed to like it especially when she smiled.) They let her walk around the grounds in the company of an orderly, and she saw that she could probably climb the fence to escape.

Later, she had taken a piece of clear plastic tape from one of the recreation rooms, and while her door was open during dinner, taped back the bolt to the lock, allowing her to re-open the door after the night orderly only carelessly closed it. A few minutes before midnight she made her way unseen down the hall and out the rear exit.

It wasn't that the hospital was an evil place, she thought. In fact, what she had seen there convinced her that it did indeed offer exceptional care. Its patients, who suffered from a wide range of debilitating conditions, both physical and mental, were provided with every necessity and many luxuries.

But in Jill's case, somebody had provided the hospital staff with misinformation. And, worse, she was being misled about her father. He had never come to see her. Instead, she had received daily messages, sent by his company and taken by the hospital's switchboard operator, that he was being detained in the field because of a minor emergency and would come to see her as soon as the problem cleared up.

It made no sense, but it was obvious to Jill that someone was lying to the hospital administrators in an attempt to keep her locked up so she would be prevented from finding out what had happened to her father. And equally obvious to her now was that the source of those lies could only be Magnum Gas, Inc., her father's employer.

It all began with them, she thought. Her father could not have been in the field performing seismological testing, as they said he was, at the same time that he was involved in an automobile wreck with her. They'd have to think she was crazy to believe something like that!

She ripped away another piece of the gown that had become snared by a runner of sawbriar and groaned, thinking about it. What if she really was crazy? Didn't crazy people think they were sane, too — as sane as she thought she was? And wasn't it true that crazy people often believed others were lying to them or concealing something from them?

She saw lights ahead of her and froze in fear that the hospital staff had already discovered she was missing and were out in force to find her. Then she realized it was only a car rounding a curve of the highway. A few minutes later, she came out of the woods and onto the shoulder.

She began running along the side of the road. When she could no longer run, she jogged, and when she could no longer jog, she walked. Then, when she was rested enough, she began running again.

There was little traffic along the mountainous road, and she avoided the few cars that did appear, ducking into the cover of the woods as soon as she saw headlights. Clothed in little more than her underthings, she did not think that being found running almost naked in the middle of the night would do much to support her claim that she didn't need to be locked up for her own good.

\*　\*　\*

It was a long, arduous haul, and dawn was breaking when she finally reached her house on the country road outside Center Ridge. She had come more than fifteen miles, and she was nearly exhausted, but, before entering the darkened house, she hid at the edge of the woods another ten minutes to be sure no one was waiting for her.

The door was unlocked from when they had fled that night, and inside, everything was just as she had last seen it. Her pajamas lay in a rumpled heap on her unmade bed, and the drawer that contained her socks was ajar, her father having hurried her so to get dressed and come with him that she had neglected to close it.

Passing the full-length mirror on the bathroom door, she

41

was shocked at her appearance. She was covered with mud and dirt up to her knees, her hair was tangled and matted, and her legs and arms were crisscrossed with sawbriar scratches.

Hurrying, she drew a bath as hot as she could stand and eased herself down into it. The steaming water felt so good to her fatigued body that it brought tears to her eyes. She wanted to stay there forever. If she had closed her eyes, she would have fallen asleep right in the bathtub, but she knew she couldn't dare allow herself such a luxury.

Using plenty of soap, she scrubbed until every scratch was stinging. She shampooed her hair and half-combed, half-jerked on it, until it lay wet and straight to her shoulders. Dressing in a pair of jeans, T-shirt, and another pair of sneakers, she headed for her father's study.

She knew relatively little about Magnum Gas Company. The corporation's headquarters occupied a large, multistoried building at the state capital, but its main field office was located at Center Ridge, which was her father's base of operations.

From there, he headed up a team of technicians and workers who went out into the field and, through a variety of scientific methods and tests, determined the status of what was beneath the surface of the earth and how it related to the production of natural gas, which MGC sold into the national network of natural gas pipelines.

That was about all she knew, except that the company was reputed to be highly successful and had outbid several competing companies for the services of her father, who was considered one of the gas industry's top geologists.

Jill had no idea of what she was looking for, and she didn't find anything she considered especially useful to her. Her father's desk mainly contained samples of his routine work — data sheets, computer print-outs with notations in the margins, and various study summaries.

She found a picture taken of her father at one of the field camps and paused to look at it. He was smiling her favorite smile, and his face looked as if he hadn't shaved for at least a week. In the background were some of the portable buildings he and his men used for quarters and where they conducted their studies, and there were several pieces of heavy construction equipment. Seeing his picture brought a lump to her throat and lifted her level of concern for his safety another notch.

Going through the remaining drawers and files, Jill found a topographical map and spread it out on top of the desk. Again, it told her nothing she considered useful, but it did give her a good overall picture of Magnum Gas Company's production facilities. The map showed all of the range of Ouachita Mountains and the Patawa Preservation Area but also included the New Madrid Basin, which adjoined them.

The New Madrid Basin was a land area of several hundred square miles that formed a broad depression on the face of the earth, and on the map it was dotted with symbols that represented Magnum Gas wellheads. Magnum Gas owned the mineral rights within the New Madrid Basin, which was reputed to hold one of the country's richest supplies of natural gas. It was somewhere out there that Magnum Gas claimed her father was presently working.

Picking up the phone, Jill dialed MGC's office in Center

Ridge. When the company operator came on the line, she asked for Dr. Nathan Faraday and was told that he was in the field and was unavailable.

"Could you possibly connect me through by radio," Jill requested.

After a pause, a man's voice came on the line and said pleasantly, "Hello, may I help you?"

"I'm trying to reach Dr. Faraday," Jill said. "Can you arrange a radio patch for me?"

"He's very busy right now," the pleasant voice replied. "We have a rather involved situation going on at one of our well sites."

"This is an emergency," Jill said.

"If you'll give me your name and the nature of the emergency, I'll see that he gets the message as quickly as possible."

Hoping she hadn't given herself away, Jill hung up the phone. She had heard enough to know that she wasn't going to get anything but a runaround, and she knew anyway that she needed help from someone with authority to get the answers she wanted from Magnum Gas. If she could get to Kennethville, she could catch a bus to the capital and get in touch with the State Gas Commission — and the FBI, too, if necessary.

Though she was fatigued, being tired could not be allowed to matter, she decided. Stopping in the kitchen only long enough to make and swallow half a peanut butter sandwich and wash it down with some milk, she went to the carport, where she filled the tank of one of the trail bikes and kick-started the two-wheeler to life. Any minute now, the people at the hospital would be checking her room and discovering that the sleeping shape under the bed covers was only an arrangement of pillows.

Opening the throttle and toeing the bike through its gears, she shot out of the carport and headed down the road.

Going up on the pegs when she needed to, she rode fast and hard, controlling the bike with the same kind of natural ability that had made piloting an airplane come so easily to her. But as she neared the curve where she and her father had been forced from the road by the blinding light, she slowed. Something on the shoulder caught her eye, and she brought the bike to an abrupt, sliding stop.

With a feeling approaching elation, she recognized the object as soon as she had a better look at it. It was a small aluminum muffler with the dual tail pipes still attached, and there was no way it could have come from any of the local pickup trucks or four-wheel-drive vehicles. The manufacturer's stamp on it clearly indicated that it belonged to an imported sports car like her father's.

"Proof!" she said out loud as she strapped the muffler to the back of her bike with the bungy cords that were attached to the wire rack. "They'll have to believe me now!"

# 7.

CODY HAD BEEN TO KENNETHVILLE OFTEN ENOUGH TO know his way around there fairly well, and he didn't have much trouble in locating the office, which had a small parking lot in front and a sign hanging from chains that said "J. N. Boxley, Attorney at Law." It was shady where he stopped the truck, so he let Riley out of the cab and ordered him into the back, from where the setter could watch and smell the workings of civilization and maybe succeed in conning a passerby into stopping for a minute to rub his ears.

"Now don't give me any trouble, Riley, okay?" Cody said. "Just stay there."

Riley thumped his tail, and Cody went on inside. He had never gone to see a lawyer before, and the idea already had him feeling a little intimidated. The plush carpet and the elegant-looking furniture and the very professional appearance of the receptionist didn't make him feel any more comfortable about it, either.

"May I help you?" the receptionist asked.

"My name is Cody Burke," Cody said.

"Oh yes," she replied, smiling now and looking at her appointment book. "You're a few minutes early. If you'll have a seat, Mr. Boxley will see you shortly."

Cody looked around and then sat down at one end of a long couch and continued to feel uneasy. It must have been the receptionist who had phoned his home this morning, he decided. He had been worried ever since his mother gave him the message that a lawyer wanted to see him about a matter concerning Joe Tiotec.

Joe Tiotec had been dead now for three days, and Cody couldn't imagine what the attorney wanted. It couldn't have anything to do with a will, because Joe hadn't owned anything worth leaving to anybody. Even the small plot of land and the cabin that he had long ago inherited from his mother would not be passed on, because Joe had provided that it become state property as part of the Patawa Preservation on his death.

So if it couldn't be about a will, what could it be about? Cody wondered. After a man's death, what else was left that would involve an attorney?

"Mr. Boxley will see you now," the receptionist said, and Cody got up quickly and headed through the door that she indicated.

Boxley stood up behind his desk and offered Cody his hand. He was a plump-faced man, in his thirties, and Cody was glad to see that he didn't seem as intimidating as the atmosphere of his office suggested.

"Joe Tiotec told me that you were an exceptional young man," Boxley said after Cody was seated. "He said you helped him in his field work and research."

"I didn't do very much," Cody replied.

Boxley nodded thoughtfully, as if he was thinking that the modest statement was what Joe Tiotec had led him to expect from the muscular, good-looking youngster. "I'm sure you're wondering why I asked you to come here."

"Yes, I am," Cody admitted.

"I assume you know that Joe Tiotec's body was cremated yesterday."

"I knew that he had made arrangements to have that done," Cody said.

"Yes. He made them through me. His instructions were that there was to be no ceremony, just — just the, uh, disposal."

Cody nodded. He knew this.

"But the people at the crematorium have certain rules they follow," the lawyer added, reaching into a drawer of his desk and withdrawing a thick legal envelope. "So this goes to you."

Cody took the envelope and bent back the hasp, opening the flap. Inside was a sealed plastic bag, filled with a grayish, powdery substance and several hard chunks of something a few shades lighter in color than the rest of it.

"Joe Tiotec's ashes," Boxley said. "And this is for you, too."

He handed Cody a regular-sized envelope, and Cody opened it, withdrawing a short, handwritten note.

In Joe Tiotec's precise penmanship, the note read, "I'm sorry to stick you with this final chore, Cody. The crematorium requires that my remains be turned over to someone, and for an inexplicable quirk of personality, I hesitate to assign them to strangers. So the burden falls on you. It doesn't matter what you do with them. Use your imagination if you like." The note was signed "Joe," and dated three months earlier.

"He was a most unusual man," the attorney said.

Cody nodded. He turned the plastic bag in his hands and watched the dry ash and bone fragments spill over into an air pocket in a corner of the bag. It was hard for him to relate what he saw with the living form of Joe Tiotec that he remembered. He looked up at the attorney.

"What — what should I do with them?"

"Whatever you want. It's up to you."

"Are there any laws about it?"

"No, not in this state. Cremation is so new here that so far there aren't any regulations concerning disposal of the ashes. You can bury them or scatter them or keep them in a jar — whatever you decide."

Whatever I decide, Cody thought as he let Riley back into the cab of his truck. Maybe he would take the ashes and bury them somewhere near the Patawa River. That way, according to the beliefs of the Patawa Indians, he would almost be fulfilling the duty of bearer of Joe's spirit. That seemed like a good idea and was certainly worth considering.

When they were stopped at a traffic light, Cody held the envelope with the bag of ashes in it out to Riley. The big red setter sniffed it but without much curiosity, then turned away to get in a quick bark at a fat terrier with spindly legs in the car next to them.

"You don't recognize it as Joe, either, do you, boy?" Cody

said, and Riley thumped his tail and got in another bark at the terrier before being told to shut up.

On the drive to Kennethville, Cody had seen the beautiful Stearman biplane pass overhead again, angling down from the mountain top and sliding through the air above the Patawa Valley, and now, as he approached the airport on the way out of town, he heard music from loudspeakers and saw that a large, festive crowd had gathered on the concrete apron in front of the hangar.

When he got nearer, he heard the crowd applaud and cheer, and then he saw a pair of radio-controlled model airplanes doing loops and rolls in the air above one end of the runway. Immediately fascinated, Cody turned into the airport's parking lot and drove under a sign that said SOUTH-WEST REGIONAL FLY-OFF. RADIO-CONTROLLED MODEL AIR-CRAFT. Sponsored by Magnum Gas Company, Inc., the Energy Company with Your Future in Mind.

Ordering Riley to stay beside him in the heel position, Cody walked rapidly toward the crowd. Even the idea of model airplanes was enough to make his heart quicken with excitement. Any machine capable of flight, regardless of its size, could automatically hook his attention.

The crowd was almost as large as the one at the county fair, when the carney came to town. There were refreshment stands and several displays, where manufacturers advertised radio-controlled models and their related electronics and hardware. To Cody, all of it was interesting, but what he really wanted was to see something fly.

Working his way through the crowd (and with Riley staying obediently at his heels), Cody reached the roped-off area, beyond which sat dozens and dozens of model airplanes, most of them scaled-down reproductions of real aircraft. Beside the runway, controls in hand, owners of the aircraft waited in turn to demonstrate their skills as earthbound pilots.

A P-51, with a wingspan of almost five feet, taxied into position, made a short run as its owner opened the throttle, and lifted off. Behind it came an exact scale copy of a Boeing P-12. Both planes climbed steeply, then went into a series of acrobatic maneuvers that made the crowd *ooh* and *aah* and applaud almost continuously.

Momentarily released from the gloom he had felt since Joe Tiotec's death, Cody watched as intently as everyone else. After several minutes, the two planes landed, each getting a resounding ovation from the crowd, and two more took to the air to begin their performances. Over the loudspeaker, an emcee announced the owners' names and the manufacturers of the planes' engines and electronics.

Walking along the ropes, Cody looked from the models on the ground to those in the air, trying to take in everything at once. At the end of the roped-off area and just beyond the hangar, the ground sloped downward to the main length of the runway, and on the close-cropped grass beside the strip was the blue-and-yellow Stearman. Cody's heart nearly stopped when he saw it.

He immediately forgot everything else. Here was the plane he had been seeing in the air almost daily for nearly two weeks! Hurrying down the slope, he approached the Stearman with a sense of awe.

On close inspection, the plane was every bit as beautiful as it had been when he had only caught glimpses of it from the

51

surface of the Patawa River. The workmanship of its restoration was flawless. Even the interiors of the two open cockpits had been finished to perfection. Someone had spent a lot of time and money on this plane, and stuck in the ground beside it was an expensively lettered sign that explained.

"This classic aircraft is part of a larger collection held in public trust by Magnum Gas Company, Inc., the energy company with your future in mind."

And at the bottom of the sign, it said, "Rides to the public — $10."

Cody felt like kicking himself. All the time that he had been seeing the Stearman, it had been over here to promote this show. And he could have had a ride for only $10!

A couple of younger kids were eyeing the plane curiously and Cody asked them, "Are they still offering rides?"

"Far as I know, they are," one of them replied.

"Where's the pilot?" Cody asked.

"Eatin' lunch, I think," the kid said. "Ought to be back any minute though. You goin' up?"

"I sure am," Cody said, and then another thought suddenly struck him. The plane would carry him out over the Patawa Preservation Area. "Look," he said to the two kids, "if the pilot gets back before I do, you tell him to wait — he's got a passenger!"

It seemed to take forever for him to work his way through the crowd, but it actually took only a few minutes to return to his truck. There, he removed the plastic bag containing Joe Tiotec's ashes from the legal envelope and put it inside his shirt.

He would have left Riley in the back of the truck, but it

was parked in the direct sun, and the long-haired dog suffered from the intense summer heat. So, with the red setter trailing behind him and his heart racing in anticipation of his first airplane ride, Cody hurriedly retraced his steps through the crowd to the Stearman.

# 8.

Sheriff Jackson was reading the morning paper at his desk, when Jill entered the small brick building that served as both his office and the Oak Ridge jailhouse. He was leaning back with his feet propped up on the windowsill, and he had barely realized someone had come into the room before she clunked the muffler down on his desk.

"Look!" she said.

The sheriff looked. He looked up at her, and then he looked at the muffler on his desk. Lumps of dirt had broken off from the muffler, and the dirt was on his desk, too.

"Do you know what this is?" Jill asked.

Sheriff Jackson looked up at her and then down at his desk again. "A muffler? From an automobile?"

"Not *a* muffler. *The* muffler. The muffler from my father's car!"

The sheriff looked up at her again. He smiled at her in a strange way and raised his eyebrows, stretching his already long face. "The muffler from your father's car," he repeated.

54

"Yes!" she said excitedly. "It got knocked off the night we had the wreck, just a little before the light made us go off the road!"

"Oh yes — the wreck that you and your father had," the sheriff said. "I believe the light was in the sky, wasn't it?"

"Yes! And you couldn't find my father or the car. But now —"

"Now you've found it," he said, looking down at the muffler again.

"No! I didn't find the car, but I found this! I found the muffler!"

"You found the muffler," he repeated slowly. "You found the muffler to your father's car. Where did you find it?"

"I just told you!" she said, exasperated with his slowness to grasp what she was talking about. "I found it alongside the road, right where it was knocked off when we were trying to get away from the light!"

"It came off because you were trying to get away from the light in the sky?" the sheriff said.

"It came off because we hit a rock!" She pointed down at the muffler. "Look! You see that dent! That's where it hit the rock!"

He looked up at her and smiled. "Well, it sure does look like it was hit by something, and if you say it was a rock, then I reckon I'll have to believe you. How are you feeling, Miss — Miss Faraday, isn't it?"

"Jill Faraday," she said, "and I feel fine. Sheriff, will you listen to me?"

"You look fine, too," he said, smiling at her. "I'm glad to see that you've been released from the hospital."

"I wasn't exactly released," she said. "I more or less released myself, because they had no right to keep me there. Look, Sheriff, I know it sounds like I'm crazy, but I'm not. Everything I told you was the truth. It actually happened — just as I said it did. There was a light, and it —" She put her hand to her head. She had said all this before. Why was she having to say it again? She began to get angry. "I don't know what's going on, Sheriff, and I don't know why. But something has happened to my father, and somebody has made it look like I don't know what I'm talking about, but I *do* know what I'm talking about —"

"Now, Miss Faraday, I don't think you should upset yourself. There's no reason for you to be getting all excited."

"There's plenty of reason to get excited!" she said, her voice rising in frustration and anger. "Why won't you listen to me? Can't you understand? I'm trying to tell you that something has happened to my father, and I have proof now!" She pointed at the muffler. "It's right there in front of you. And I think Magnum Gas is responsible."

The sheriff looked down at his desk again and said thoughtfully, "You found this muffler by the road, and somehow that proves that Magnum Gas has done something with your father. Miss Faraday, people lose mufflers all the time on that old road. This could be anybody's muffler, anybody's at all."

Jill tried to control herself. It took an effort. She shook her head. "That muffler is from an imported car — like my father's."

"Everybody's car is imported nowadays, Miss Faraday. Why, half the cars in all of Farah County were made by the

Japanese." He smiled a patient smile, then said, "Look, Miss Faraday, why don't you have a seat over there and let me give Green Meadows a call. I bet those folks are worried about you, and I'm sure they'll be more than glad to send a car down to pick you up."

Jill felt herself going numb. She could hardly believe what she heard. Finding the muffler had so excited her that she had badly misjudged the effect it would have on the sheriff. Stopping here had been a serious mistake. She was just about to be redelivered to Green Meadows.

"Just a second, Sheriff. I have something else," she said and turned and walked away as if she were going to get something. But what she wanted "just a second" for was to get out of there. Going out the front door, she saw the sheriff pick up his phone.

Outside, she kicked the bike to life, spun it around in plain view in front of the Sheriff's Office, and went screaming back down the road in the same direction she had come — back toward Center Ridge. But two miles out of town, she turned off the road and stopped in a stand of pine trees. She killed the engine and waited.

Within five minutes, the sheriff's car came cruising along, obviously looking for her. As soon as it passed, she came back onto the road and reversed directions again, retracing her route through Oak Flats and turning onto the asphalt highway to Kennethville. With the whiny trail bike running flat-out at forty miles an hour, she was going to need some luck to reach there and get on the bus before they found her.

*   *   *

For a while, everything went as well as she could have hoped. The cars she encountered on the road went by without taking special notice of her, and she passed part of the time rehearsing what she would say to the State Police, the State Gas Commission, the State Department of Criminal Investigation, the FBI and anyone else who would listen to her. One of those authorities would at least make the effort to check things out before sending her back to Green Meadows, and they would see that something was wrong.

Then we'll get some answers out of Magnum Gas, Jill thought, as she approached the outskirts of Kennethville.

Ahead of her, traffic was beginning to concentrate, and for the first time, she had to slow down. Cars were turning off the highway into the local airport, and she could see that the area between the hangar and the beginning of the runway was jammed with people. A pair of radio-controlled model planes banked overhead, and Jill remembered that today was the day Magnum Gas sponsored a regional competition for RC hobbyists. It was part of MGC's overall public relations effort, and she and her father had discussed attending it.

Police were directing traffic, and Jill's lane of cars was stopped. Instinctively, she moved in close to the car ahead of her. The trail bike was not licensed for use on the highway, and she was immediately apprehensive that the police would stop her, even if they hadn't yet been alerted by the sheriff at Oak Flats.

Then she glanced back, and her apprehension was replaced by a sudden stab of fear. The front end of a dark limousine was coming up behind her, and she recognized it immediately. She whipped out onto the shoulder and moved forward along the line of traffic, stopping several cars up from where she had been.

The limousine came to a stop, and Jill saw the nurse from Green Meadows sitting in front. The nurse pointed toward her, and then the driver got out and came up the line of cars, walking quickly at first, then breaking into a run.

Jill put the trail bike in gear and shot forward again, passing more cars. As she approached the point where the police were directing traffic, she saw one of the officers spot her and alert another policeman standing beside him. From their reactions, she had no doubt that they had been informed to watch out for her.

A whistle blew, and all traffic came to a halt. One of the policemen saw that she was going to run for it, and he stepped out into the opposite lane to try to stop her.

Jill cut to her left and accelerated, continuing up the line of cars. Blowing his whistle and waving both arms, the policeman tried to head her off, but Jill swerved hard to one side and raced past him.

Angling off the side of the road, she went down into the drainage ditch and up the other side, running parallel to the fence that enclosed the airport. A police car was on the shoulder ahead of her, and she knew she couldn't get past it. With no other place left to go, she leaned the bike into a turn and zipped into the airport parking lot.

Weaving in and out of parked cars, she went the length of the lot and back, then lay the bike down in a slide of gravel behind a refreshment stand. Her helmet was another liability now, making her easy to identify. Jerking it from her head, she rolled it under the nearest car.

59

As she slipped into the crowd, she looked back and saw them coming — two policemen, followed by the big man in a dark suit who had driven the limousine.

Saying, "Excuse me, excuse me," she squirmed through the crowd and fled without any idea of where she was going. A couple of minutes later, she broke out of the crowd on the far side of the hangar and saw the open expanse of airstrip beyond. Just below her was a restored Stearman, one of the grand old classics that she knew belonged to the Magnum Gas Company's aviation collection.

A shrill whining noise split the air, and simultaneously the crowd released a collective expression of awe. Jill turned to see a jet-powered model of an F-16 rocketing into the sky and was nearly knocked down by two kids running up from the direction of the Stearman to get a better look.

While everyone's attention was on the F-16, Jill walked quickly down the slope toward the staggerwing Stearman. She crossed to the other side of the biplane and stood there, looking back over the rear part of the fuselage.

Maybe no one will think to look for me here, she thought, and then she saw the old aviator's cap left by the step-up on the lower wing. Quickly she pulled it over her head and stuffed her hair up in it.

Seen from the direction of the crowd, she would be feet and jeans below the fuselage of the Stearman, and above it she hoped she would be the head of an old-time aviator, not the face and hair of the teenage girl her pursuers were looking for.

# 9.

When he heard the f-16 come shrilly to life, Cody had to stop for a moment to watch the plane perform. But even the incredible aerobatics of the model fighter could not hold him for long. With Riley at his heels, he hurried on through the crowd.

When he saw the Stearman, he also saw the head with the aviator's cap on the other side of it, and he felt lucky that the pilot had already returned. With everyone else interested in the performances of the model planes, maybe he wouldn't have to wait to ride in the biplane, he thought.

Going around the tail section of the Stearman, he approached the person he assumed was the pilot.

"Oh," he said, when she turned around, "you're a girl."

Jill barely glanced at him. Her attention was on the crowd. "Should I apologize?"

"No, of course not," Cody replied, the words sounding clumsy to him as they came out. "I just didn't expect — well,

I don't know what I expected. But you're not any older than I am."

"That's my father's fault," Jill said without taking her eyes from the crowd. "He was too busy to meet my mother when he should have. Otherwise, I'd be a lot older." Whoever this guy was, she wished he would leave. What did he want anyway?

She was obviously something of a smart aleck, Cody thought, and it made him feel awkward that she didn't look at him when she spoke. But he didn't want to offend her. "I only meant that you seemed, well, young for a pilot."

Jill glanced quickly at him again and saw that he really did think she was the pilot of this plane. It gave her a very small feeling of security. If this guy thought she was the pilot, then maybe the people looking for her might think so, too, and not pay special attention to the figures standing beside the Stearman.

"I've been flying since nearly before I could walk," she said. "My father taught me. He's flown almost everything that has wings."

A policeman came out of the crowd and looked in the direction of the Stearman. Jill's heart almost stopped beating. Then he looked back at the throng of people and began walking along the edge of them.

"Are you waiting for someone?" Cody asked.

"Uh, no," she said, turning to look at him and the red setter that was sitting obediently at his heels.

"Then you can take me up now?"

"Well, I —" She looked up at the crowd again and saw the big man in the dark suit. Hardly noticing the Stearman at

62

all, he began circling the crowd in the opposite direction. She turned back to Cody and saw that he was holding out a ten-dollar bill. "What's that for?"

"For my fare — for the ride," he said, wondering why she asked that, when the sign said it was ten dollars.

"Oh, well, you don't pay until afterwards," she said.

"Fine. I'll take my dog up there," he said, pointing toward the hangar, "and then I'll be right back."

Jill turned her scrutiny back on the crowd but also noticed as Cody led the red setter up to the shade at the side of the hangar and told him to stay there. She was wondering what she would do with this guy when he returned, when suddenly the nurse from Green Meadows appeared out of the crowd and stopped at the edge of the hangar apron to look around.

Jill knew that of the people pursuing her the nurse would know better than anyone else what she looked like, and the aviator's cap was probably inadequate as a disguise. Trying to appear casual, Jill turned her back.

"Okay," Cody said, returning to the plane, "I'm ready."

"Uh, yes." Jill glanced over the fuselage of the Stearman toward the crowd again. The nurse was looking directly at them, and it took all of Jill's self-control to keep from breaking and running for it. The only other thing to do was to act natural, play out the charade and hope the nurse bought it.

"Which cockpit is mine?" Cody asked, eager to get in.

"Uh, the rear one," Jill replied. She pointed to the step-up on the lower wing. "Put your foot there."

Cody stepped onto the wing and then over into the cockpit, sitting down in the deep seat with the joystick and instrumentation in front of him and the small windshield rising just a little above the level of his eyes. From inside, the plane felt larger and sturdier than he had imagined.

Another aviator's cap was hung on the stick, and Jill reached inside the cockpit and handed it to him. While he put it on, she brought the straps over his shoulders and snapped them into place, securing him in the seat. She risked another glance, hoping that the nurse had seen enough of the routine of two people getting into an airplane and had gone elsewhere to look for her, but the woman was still there, and she was looking at them a little too curiously to suit Jill. And then there was something else to contend with.

"No, Riley! No!" Cody said angrily. "I told you to stay!"

The dog had seen his master getting into the airplane, and he felt compelled enough to investigate it that he had disobeyed. Now he reared up and put his big front paws on the side of the fuselage in an attempt to look in and see where the part of Cody's body below his neck had gone.

"No, Riley! No!" Cody said in his stearnest voice, and Riley dropped to the ground, backed up a few steps, sat, barked twice and began howling long, plaintive howls, one right after the other.

"Oh, for th— Riley, stop that!" Cody said. "No! Stop it!"

Riley thumped his tail, then threw his head back, howling again.

The nurse had started to turn away, but now the howls caught her attention, as they did the attentions of several other people, and suddenly Jill was more vulnerable than ever.

"What's the matter with your stupid dog?" she asked angrily. "Can't you shut him up? He's making a spectacle of us!"

"I'm sorry," Cody said. "Sometimes he — he's just . . ."

"Do something!" she snapped, as Riley threw back his head and howled a howl that she thought should have ruptured his throat. "Make him stop that!"

"No, Riley! No!" Cody tried to come up out of the cockpit to discipline him, but he was strapped in, and he was unfamiliar with the fastener. He fumbled clumsily with it.

Oh Lord, Jill thought. Just what I needed — some nut and his psychotic dog. She glanced up at the crowd. Everybody she saw was looking at them, and the person looking most intently was the nurse. And now the crazy dog was going crazier. Rearing up, he put his front paws on the fuselage again and began a frenzy of barking that was so loud it made the wires between the Stearman's wings twang.

In utter frustration, Jill stepped down from the wing and grabbed the dog by his rear quarters, picking him up.

"If he wants his master that bad, then let's give him what he wants," she said, shoving him on up and over, dumping him into the cockpit with Cody.

Instantly, Riley shut up. He came down on top of Cody with his eyes wide and his legs stiff and rigid. The excitement was suddenly no longer fun. He didn't like being dumped into unfamiliar places, and he hooked the claws of his big feet into any purchase he could find. One of the purchases was Cody's left ear.

"Hey! What are you doing?" Cody said, objecting.

"Giving you your dog!"

"This isn't going to work!" he said, his face full of Riley's long chest hair. "There isn't room for both of us!"

"Who cares," she said, and suddenly she really didn't

65

care — about anything. There was no way she could fight this kind of rotten luck, where one insane dog could turn her entire escape attempt into an exercise of slapstick. She started just to walk away, and then she thought, Well, let them come and get me. I'm not going to go to them.

Stepping upon the wing again, she climbed over into the forward cockpit. Sitting down, she looked toward the crowd of people, most of whom were still gawking in the direction of the Stearman. In the aft cockpit, the dog's four legs were sticking up, as Cody tried to shift him around and out of his lap. That was what most of the people were looking at — except for the nurse. The nurse was looking right at Jill, and when she turned into the crowd, Jill knew that she was going after the policemen and the big man in the dark suit.

Well, they'll have to pry me out of here, she thought, slumping down in the seat.

In the aft cockpit, Cody gradually worked Riley over to one side, wedging him on his back between him and the inside of the fuselage. The setter's eyes now looked twice their normal size, and he was liking the arrangement about as much as Cody was.

"Look," Cody said, "I think my dog and I want to get out of the plane." What he was really thinking was that the FAA should review this pilot's mental condition before they renewed her license next time. There was something funny about the way she was acting — as if she didn't have everything together in her head.

Jill hardly noticed what he was saying. Until this very moment, she had regarded the plane as nothing more than a stage prop — something merely to conceal her from the people who wanted to take her back to Green Meadows. That she had not considered the possibility of flying it was simply because she was a competent pilot, and part of being a competent pilot meant not flying anything you weren't checked out in first.

But now, as she looked at the instrumentation and overhead at the clear line bringing fuel down from the tanks, she realized that this plane was about as simple and basic as an airplane could be, and the odds were that she could fly it. In fact, she had even flown a tail-dragger before, a Pitts. Her father had been with her, and the Pitts was smaller and lighter than this old Stearman was, but it was also similar in that it was a biplane with a joystick.

"I said I think we'll be getting out," Cody repeated and tried to get the strap unfastened, only to have Riley's legs fall over into his lap again.

Jill switched on the ignition and hit the starter.

The big radial engine coughed twice, then exploded to life.

Riley thought he was being eaten by whatever he had been thrown inside of, and he jerked around in Cody's lap, hooking him with his feet and holding to him in absolute terror.

"I've changed my mind!" Cody shouted. "I don't want to ride with you!"

Jill opened the throttle a little more, and the Stearman began to break from its resting place. She moved the stick and felt the plane respond to the prop wash over its elevator.

"We want out!" Cody yelled.

Jill could hardly hear him over the roar of the engine, but she wasn't concerned with him anyway. Out of the crowd came the big man in the dark suit, followed by the two policemen. When they saw the plane begin to move, they broke into a run.

Jill opened the throttle more, and the big Stearman lumbered for the runway. Then, when its tires touched the asphalt, it picked up speed quickly and she nearly ran off the other side before getting down enough right pedal to turn it.

The sharp swerving of the airplane helped to throw Riley out of Cody's lap and wedge him against the inside of the fuselage again, and Cody looked out in horror as the aircraft veered from one side of the runway to the other. Looking back, he saw a big man run up to the tail of the plane and catch the trailing edge of the rudder.

"Stop!" Cody shouted at her. "They want you to stop! I want you to stop! Stop!"

Jill felt the man grab the rudder. As he was dragged, his weight helped correct her overcontrol of the pedals and actually aided her in getting the plane pointed down the runway. She gave the Stearman full throttle, and there was no way the man could hold on. In the rearview mirror above her, she saw him slip away and fall, rolling on the asphalt through the blast of prop wash. She also saw the expression on her passenger's face. She had never seen anybody look like that.

The Stearman gained speed rapidly. Jill pulled back on the stick, and the powerful radial hauled the plane into the air seemingly without effort. The grand old aircraft was rock solid and steady, like nothing she had ever flown before. She moved the stick over, and they went into a climbing bank that turned the landscape and shrank the airport below them to nothingness.

# 10.

Each time Cody managed to get Riley out of his lap, the setter managed to get back there again. Bug-eyed with fear, the ninety-pound dog showed an amazing ability to use his feet in times of desperation, becoming especially adept at hooking his claws onto the straps that held Cody to the seat.

Finally, in utter frustration, Cody grabbed the loose skin of the dog's cheeks with both hands and snatched Riley's face up into his own, until their noses were almost touching.

"I said stop it, Riley!" he said in double his most threatening tone. "And I mean stop it, do you hear me?" He gave the dog's head another shake. "Don't you stick your feet on me again!"

Riley's eyes rolled fearfully, but the shaking and the look of dead seriousness on his master's face were getting through to him. He remained rigid, but he stopped struggling and pawing for everything within reach.

One at a time, Cody disengaged himself from each of the stiff legs and worked Riley over into the narrow space beside him again, but this time he got him in there upright. When Riley's head came up into the rush of air, the sensation was enough like that of riding with his face stuck out the window of Cody's truck that it had a calming effect on him.

Looking in the rear-view mirror, Jill was relieved finally to see some order back there. During their thrashing around, she had felt them strike the control stick several times, and she had been afraid they would jam it and all three of them and the plane would end up in little pieces strewn about the countryside.

She had time for a better look at her passenger and saw that he was kind of cute, with sandy-colored hair, clean-cut features and blue eyes that were wide with fright. He was in fact scared silly. And now he began hollering at her again.

"What are you doing? What are you doing?" Cody yelled as loudly as he could, trying to make himself heard over the din of engine and air.

She cupped her mouth with one hand and yelled back at him. "I'm stealing this plane!"

"Stealing this plane?"

"Stealing this plane!" she shouted again.

"Stealing this — oh my gosh! Do you know how to fly it?"

"What do you think we're doing? Skate-boarding?"

"I mean can you land it?" he shouted. "Can you *land* this plane?"

She looked back at him and smiled. Then she shrugged. "I don't know. I've never tried it before!"

She saw him mouth the words, "Oh my —," and then she lost what he said after that, but he was speaking mainly to himself. Then he shouted again, "Where are you going?"

71

"To the state capital," she shouted back.

"That's two hundred fifty miles!"

"It's closer as the crow flies!" she replied, but she really didn't know how far it was by air. And heading in the right direction was a problem, too. The old plane did not come equipped with Omni, so she wasn't going to have the usual convenience of a radio vector to guide her to her destination. But she had looked at enough maps of the area terrain to remember some rudimentary facts.

She knew that she should be able to follow the Patawa River eastward to where it emptied into the Ouachita River and then follow the Ouachita River northward to where it was crossed by Interstate 30, which would then lead her to the capital. The distant sky was hazy with humidity, but the weather was plenty adequate for VFR, and the old plane handled much more easily than she had anticipated, so she didn't expect much trouble until she was on the ground again and had to begin explaining everything she was going to have to explain.

She looked in the mirror at Cody again and saw that he was holding both hands to his head in disbelief. By contrast, the dog appeared to be enjoying himself now. His tongue was lolling out and his jaws were open, and he seemed to like the feel of the wind beating him in the face.

But Cody could hardly believe it indeed. It seemed like a dream to him, a bad one he would very much like to awaken from. In fact, he could think of nothing more desirable than suddenly to find himself at home, in bed — safe.

This was crazy, he thought. Everything was crazy, and especially the girl, whoever she was. But if he thought she was crazy, he was also beginning to notice that she seemed to know what she was doing with the control stick. The movements of the duplicate stick in the cockpit he was sharing with Riley were measured and precise, and the plane drove its way through the air with a reassuring steadiness.

After several minutes, he began to feel cautiously optimistic that maybe there was a chance he would get out of this alive. Under other circumstances, he knew he would have enjoyed the ride. The sensations of flight were as pleasant as he had thought they would be. Looking back, he realized that they were already deep into the Patawa Preservation Area. The highway had long since disappeared into the haze behind them, and in the distance ahead lay the Patawa River, twisting and snaking through the unbroken forests of the vast preserve.

With each passing minute, Jill became more appreciative of the Stearman. It was like a tractor in the air, a workhorse of a machine, slow but powerful, with strength being at the heart of its outmoded design. It was so wonderfully overbuilt and overpowered by the huge radial engine that it would inevitably instill confidence in its pilot.

The only thing that bothered her was the status of the fuel supply. There was no gauge for that, and she could only speculate about how much was in the tanks. She was trying to reason it out, thinking that more than likely the Stearman was filled each day and probably hadn't been flown enough today to have used much fuel, when suddenly the engine sputtered and caught, sputtered and caught again, then sputtered and died.

Cody nearly came up out of his seat in spite of the straps

73

that held him there. "What is it? What's wrong? What happened to the motor?"

Quickly Jill tried to get the engine to windmill and restart. When that failed, she tried the starter again. The engine sputtered a couple of times, but that was all. In its silence remained only the accompanying sound of the wind past the fuselage and through the struts and wings.

"Get the motor started! Do it!" Cody shouted.

Jill shook her head and pointed to the clear fuel line overhead, from which the color of gasoline was now absent. "We're out of gas!"

Cody looked down. Already they were rapidly losing altitude. "We're going to crash!" he said. Then, desperately hoping there might be a chance he was wrong, he asked, "Are we going to crash?"

Jill nodded. "I think so!"

"You think so? You think so?" Cody shouted.

"I'm pretty sure about it."

"You're pretty sure about it!" he repeated. "Can't you do something?"

"Look for a place to put down!" she told him, and that shut him up for a few moments while he looked, giving her a chance to do some quick thinking.

There really wasn't any place to put down. She already knew that. As far as she could see, there was nothing but undulating mountains, covered by a carpet of trees, which were coming up fast. The heavy Stearman did not glide well at all. Without the brute power of its engine, it had little affinity for the sky.

"I don't see anything! I don't see anything!" Cody shouted.

"I'll try to make the river! It'll be better than hitting the trees!"

"Better than hitting the trees!" Cody repeated. "That's great! That's just really great!"

Jill didn't reply. Trying to keep the airspeed above stall, she put the Stearman into a steeper glide pattern. Then she began to nurse it, pulling back on the stick in an attempt to stretch the glide out to the river, which was so far away that its outline was hazy through the humid atmosphere.

That was also against their making it, she thought. Warm, humid air was less dense than cool, dry air and therefore less supportive of any airfoil flying through it. The only thing they had in their favor at all was that the terrain sloped toward the river, but that restored only a tiny fraction of the altitude the Stearman lost in the glide angle of its descent.

Cody put his arm around his dog's neck and drew him to him, but he got no comfort there. Riley was completely unconcerned. In fact, he was just now really beginning to enjoy this. Without the overbearing noise of the engine and the blast from its prop, this flying business was almost as much fun as riding in the back of Cody's truck. He pulled his head away from Cody and got his nose back into the stream of air. The woods were coming up. He could smell them.

"I want you to know something!" Cody shouted to the back of the head in front of him. "I was just looking for an airplane ride when I ran into you, and you had no right — no right! — to involve me in this! You're going to kill me, and you have no right to do that! It's not fair!"

Jill heard him, but she wasn't listening to him. She was becoming more and more doubtful that they would make it to the river, but she continued trying to stretch it out. The river was the only chance they had to gain enough room to lessen the impact. In reality, however, it came down mainly to a choice of where she decided for them to die — crashing into the trees of the mountains or against the rocks in the river.

"It's not fair!" Cody repeated, his heart pounding almost as much with anger as with fear.

"I'm sorry," she said, and she was. Without a concern personally for him at all, she had just taken him along for the ride. There was something almost criminal about that, and she regretted it.

"You're sorry!" Cody said. "Well, that's just terrific! The last words I hear in my whole life are that you're sorry!"

She didn't have time to say anything else. They had run out of room, and the trees were rushing up, their humped crowns big and intimidating. Jill pulled back more on the stick, holding the Stearman at the very edge of a stall and knowing, if it did stall, the aircraft would fall like a brick.

The river was ahead of them. She could see the water glistening in the sun immediately beyond the edge of the trees. She felt the Stearman begin to stall, and she shoved the stick forward, reaching for the winding ribbon of water. The biplane nosed downward again, swooping in.

Cody pulled Riley over into his lap and held him there. There was a sudden jolt as the undercarriage clipped a tree, and then they were over the river and going down.

Jill had no chance to get the plane lined up. They crossed the river at an angle, and with almost no response in the controls, she aimed the nose of the plane at the short gravel bar on the opposite side.

The Stearman fell out of the air. Its landing gear struck the high point of the gravel bar and collapsed. On its belly, the plane slid down the back side of the bar, cut a path through the mud of a high-water slough, continued on up the slope, and rammed its nose into the soft earth bank in the shade of the trees.

# 11.

RILEY WAS ON HIS BACK AGAIN. THE IMPACT RIPPED HIM from Cody's grip, and he was thrown past the control stick and into the bulkhead at his master's feet. Landing on his back like that hurt, and it gave him an abrupt change of mind about the pleasures of riding in an airplane. He had had enough of this.

Clawing and kicking, he scrambled to his feet, climbed right up Cody's body, and jumped from the cockpit, which was considerably closer to the ground than it had been before.

Cody was stunned. The straps had given him a severe jolt when the plane impacted, allowing his head to snap forward and back, but he was stunned mainly because he realized he was alive, which was very much a surprise.

The head in front of him was also showing signs of life, and a moment later, she looked around at him.

"Are you all right?" they asked each other simultaneously.

"I'm fine," she said.

"Just shook up is all, I think," he replied.

This time Cody managed to unfasten the harness, and he

stepped to the ground only a second or two after she did. They walked around the plane in silence, looking at it.

The airframe had not deformed, and the wings had only minor damage. The cylinder heads were partially covered by dirt that had caved off from the embankment, but the prop was not broken. Only the underside of the plane was seriously damaged. The belly landing had torn the fabric, and part of the broken landing gear had been shoved upward through the plane's skin.

"All in all, I'd say it's in pretty good shape," Cody said. "You probably shouldn't get more than twenty or thirty years for stealing it."

Jill had that numbing feeling again. This time it came with a dizzying sense of nausea and the feeling that her knees were going to buckle. She sat down quickly and bent her head forward.

"Are you sure you're all right?" Cody asked.

She nodded. "Like you said, just shook up is all. Also, I've only had a couple of bites to eat since yesterday, and I'm tired." She looked up and motioned to the plane. "And now this." She sighed. "All I needed was a little gas."

"Looks to me like you're going to need a big lawyer," Cody surmised.

"The plane belongs to Magnum Gas, and anything that happens to it is their fault," she said angrily. She bent forward again, placed her head in her hands, and realized she still had on the aviator's cap. Jerking it off, she shook out her hair and immediately felt better.

Watching her thick blonde hair fall free and frame her face and intense, blue eyes confirmed what Cody had already begun to suspect. She was remarkably pretty. But that observation was overshadowed by his earlier impression that a few of her rivets were popped. Standing up, she began working her hands through the length of her hair, and he thought he could see a kind of fire burning inside her.

"Look," she said. "I've got to get out of here, and I've got to get out of here fast. Which way do you think would be the nearest highway?"

Cody studied her a moment longer, then turned and pointed back in the direction they had come. "That way. I'd say about fifty-five miles."

"Fifty-five miles?"

"Maybe only fifty," he said, then added, "or maybe sixty."

"But that can't be!" she said, and he could see that the thought was alarming to her. "There's got to be a road closer than that!"

"There are no roads at all," he said. "You couldn't see any from the air, could you?"

"No, but I couldn't see fifty-five miles, either."

"Well, take my word for it. There aren't any roads. There aren't even any trails — except what the deer make, and those won't take you out of here. As near as I can tell, you've put us down about right smack in the middle of the Patawa Preservation Area." Cody looked out at the river. "I was through here last summer. The nearest town is Center Ridge, and that's at least an eight-to-ten-day trip — by canoe, which we don't have."

It was nearly the worst thing she could have heard. So badly did she not want it to be true that she almost started to argue with him, but there was something in his look that made her realize he probably knew what he was talking about. She felt the twin, sinking feelings of frustration and hopelessness.

"What about walking out straight through the woods?"

Cody shook his head. "It's so rough out there, you probably wouldn't make it, and even if you did, it would take weeks."

"I don't have weeks," she said. "Or ten days or eight days. I don't have any time at all!"

"Well, I have plans, too," Cody said. "And they didn't include being here right now."

"You don't understand," she said, shaking her head. "This just won't do. I can't be stranded out here. I just can't!"

"It doesn't really matter what won't do or what can't be. The only thing that matters is what is. And what is is you've got us both up a river without a paddle — or even a boat," Cody said.

Jill groaned dismally. "I can't believe they wouldn't have more fuel in the plane than that. We weren't in the air forty-five minutes."

"It looks to me like it still has gas," Cody said, looking again at the Stearman.

Jill stood up to see. The clear fuel line coming down from the tanks was now obviously full of gasoline. "But it was empty before! You saw!" she said. "I pointed it out to you!"

"I'm not sure I was seeing anything all that well," Cody replied, "except for the approaching end of my life."

"Well, it wasn't getting gas. There must have been trash in the line that jarred loose when we crashed." She groaned. "Of all the incredible luck!"

"It doesn't matter now," Cody said. "Or, if it does, all it means is the authorities won't have any reason to think we ran out of gas — which means they won't be looking for us anywhere near here."

"Oh, that's right," Jill moaned. "And they wouldn't see the plane anyway, since it's under these trees."

"That should be all right with you," Cody replied. "I think air piracy is a federal crime — not to mention kidnapping. You've probably earned the attention of every FBI agent in the state."

Jill looked directly at Cody. "Believe me, there's no place I'd rather be right now than in the hands of the FBI."

Cody didn't ask her why she said that. He wasn't sure he wanted to know. She looked reasonably normal to him, and she sounded pretty intelligent. And she had certainly known how to fly an airplane. In his mind, that was no small accomplishment. But *stealing* an airplane — that was something else indeed.

"In fact, that's where I was going," she said. "I was trying to get in touch with the FBI."

"Uh, so that's why you stole the plane?" Cody asked, trying to make his voice sound logical. "So you could reach the FBI."

"Yes and no," Jill replied. "I was going to take a bus to see the FBI, but then I had to run away from the police. That's really why I took the plane."

"Why didn't you just ask the police to get in touch with the FBI?"

"Because they wouldn't. They would have just taken me back to — back to Green Meadows Hospital."

Now some things were more clear to Cody. Having grown up in the area, he was well aware of the existence of the local "nut house" or "funny farm," which was how most of the kids he knew referred to Green Meadows. Of course, he also knew that those were simplistic and unfair labels for an institution that was reputed to offer a high quality of mental and medical health care, but the standing joke among his friends had been that whenever anyone did anything crazy it was time for them to be "sent over to Green Meadows." Well, now he had met a real, first-class resident of the place.

Jill read his reaction and said, "I know what you're thinking, but you're wrong. They locked me up there by mistake."

"Uh, yes," Cody said. "If you say so."

"You see, Magnum Gas Company did something with my father, and then they tricked the sheriff and the doctors into keeping me at Green Meadows, so I wouldn't be able to find out what they did with him."

She saw the skepticism increase in Cody's expression, but she was suddenly too tired and too full of despair to get angry or go into a long explanation about it. "It doesn't matter," she said wearily. "The only important thing is what happens now. What do we do? How do we get out of here?"

"We'll have to follow the river," Cody answered, glad to see that she wasn't so crazy she couldn't be concerned with practical matters. "It's the only sure way. We'll have to walk and wade and probably have to swim some, too."

"What about food?"

"We may get pretty hungry, but we won't starve," he assured her. "There are berries and wild onions, and we can probably manage to catch some fish."

"How long?" she asked. "How long will it take?"

Cody shook his head. "I don't know for sure. I've always traveled by canoe. I've never had to walk it before, but I'd guess at least fourteen or fifteen days."

"Fourteen or fif — oh no!" Jill sat down again, nearly collapsing onto the soft, cool earth beside the Stearman, and leaned back against the embankment. "By then it may be too late." She sighed. "It may already be too late."

No matter how nutty she may have appeared, there was no mistaking the look of total despair on her face, and Cody felt a sudden wave of sympathy for her. "Since it's more than likely that we're going to be together for a while, we might as well know each other's name," he said, holding out his hand to her. "I'm Cody Burke."

Jill reached up numbly, then was a little surprised at the feeling of strength and confidence that came with his handshake. "Jill Faraday," she replied. "I'd say I'm pleased, but under the circumstances, I don't think I'm able to be pleased about anything."

"Look," Cody said, seeing Riley lolling in the water at the edge of the river, "I'm going to go check on my dog. He came out of the plane like he was okay, but I want to make sure."

Riley was fine. He was in his favorite summertime place, letting the cool clear water swirl about his chest and belly. He stood impatiently while Cody examined him, and then he trotted over to some nearby shoals to look for fish.

Cody was turning away from the river to go back to where the girl was waiting, when he felt a sudden warmth against his side.

In all that had happened, he had completely forgotten about Joe Tiotec's ashes. He had intended to scatter them from the cockpit of the Stearman into the air above the Patawa Preservation. Reaching inside his shirt, he pulled out the plastic bag.

The bag seemed abnormally warm to him, but he dismissed that as a result of the hot day and his own body heat. For several moments, he stood looking at the ashes, thinking, and then he said aloud, "This is as good a place as any for you, Joe."

Kneeling beside the river, Cody opened the bag's seal and began sifting its contents onto the surface of the water. Some of the particles sank, and some that were hardly more than dust floated, but in only a few seconds, the last remains of the last of the Patawa Indians were swept into oblivion by the current of the river that bore their name.

From the shade beside the Stearman, Jill saw him gently shaking something from a bag into the water, but she was so tired she had little interest in what he was doing. Changing her position, she lay back and rested her head in a soft depression at the base of the embankment.

When Cody returned to the downed plane, he found her in a deep sleep. He didn't disturb her.

It was going to take so long to get out of here that it really didn't matter if they waited a while before getting started.

# 12.

She awoke feeling groggy but rested. It was night-time, but she came out of her sleep remembering full well where she was. She saw the dark hulk of the Stearman beside her and then the long, dancing shadows made by the fire that flickered invitingly on the gravel bar a short distance away.

Cody looked up when she walked into the perimeter of light. He watched her fold down into a kind of lethargic sitting position a few feet away.

"Hello," he said.

"Hi." She ran her fingers through her hair, halfheartedly trying to work out the kinks.

"You look sleepy."

"I feel better," she said. "Why did you let me sleep?"

"I figured you must have needed to. Otherwise, you wouldn't have."

She nodded and yawned. "Yeah, I guess I did need to. I see you had some matches."

"No, I found a butane lighter in a compartment of the plane. We were lucky."

She turned her head sideways and looked at him. "Lucky?"

Cody laughed. "All things considered, I mean. I also found this," he said, holding out a can of insect repellant. "I sprayed a mist of it over you while you were asleep. I hope it didn't bother you."

"It must not have, because I didn't notice." She looked at him again. "Thanks."

"You're welcome."

They were silent for several moments, and then she asked, "Where's your dog?"

"Nosing around somewhere. He's probably down at the river, looking for a muskrat or trying to catch fish."

"Fish?"

"Yeah, he has a thing for fish. He never catches any, but that doesn't stop him from trying."

"That's kind of strange for a dog, isn't it?"

"I guess, but then Riley's kind of a strange dog. You can never be sure what he's going to do."

"Like howling," she suggested.

"Yeah, that's a good example. I don't know what got into him back at the airport, but every now and then he'll do something crazy just to give me a lot of trouble, I think."

Jill stretched her arms out and yawned again. The night air was pleasant, and the fire gave just enough warmth. Her stomach growled so loud that both of them heard it.

"Boy!" she said, a little embarrassed. "You didn't happen to find a couple of Big Macs and an order of fries in the plane, too, did you?"

Cody shook his head and laughed. "No. In fact, I didn't do very well in the food department at all. I sharpened a stick and tried to spear us a fish, but this isn't a good place for that. I should have better luck a little farther downstream. In the meantime, this is all I was able to find." He held out a section of vine with clusters of small, round fruit dangling from it. "Muscadines."

"Muscadines?"

"Wild grapes," he said. "But they're not ripe yet, so —"

He warned her too late. She had already popped one in her mouth, and when she bit down on it, the sourness nearly turned her cheeks inside out.

"Wow!" she said, when she was able to make her mouth work again. "I think I'm going to have to get a lot hungrier before I can eat those!"

"There are plenty of other things to eat along the river," Cody said. "I would have gone farther in looking for something, but I was afraid you might wake up and think I had abandoned you."

She looked at him again, curious about him. "That's nice of you."

Cody shrugged. "Most people don't realize how rugged this country is. You don't want to be left out here by yourself, unless you know what you're doing."

Jill didn't have to ask him if he knew what he was doing. His quiet manner exuded a kind of confidence she could feel, and she sensed that he was in his element, as comfortable sitting Indian-style by the fire as she might have been stretched out on the couch in her own living room.

"The idea of fish sounds good to me," she said. "I like fish. In fact, a baked filet of sole, drenched in lemon-and-butter sauce, would do really nicely right about now."

Cody laughed again. He had been afraid when she woke up that he would have a raging psychopath on his hands, but she seemed to be trying to be cheerful, and he appreciated that. He was about to tell her she should probably lower her expectations from filet of sole in lemon-butter to maybe a perch cooked in its own juices, when suddenly he had a strange feeling.

Jill detected the change in his expression and saw his eyes dart to the darkness in the direction of the river.

"What is it?" she asked.

He motioned her quiet with one hand and listened intently. There was a stillness he had not noticed earlier, and he felt it descend over them like a cloak.

"I don't hear anything," she said nervously.

"Neither do I," he replied. "And that's what's wrong."

Out of the silence came the plinking sound of a loose stone, and then Riley entered the circle of yellow light. He stood dripping wet in front of Cody and wagged his tail in triumph. Clamped between his jaws was a brown bass, a good one, about two pounds.

"I thought you said he never catches any fish," Jill said.

"He doesn't," Cody answered, getting to his feet.

Ignoring his dog, Cody walked out into the darkness toward the river.

"Hey, don't leave me here!" Jill said, getting up quickly and following him.

Walking across the gravel bar, they gradually grew accustomed to the lesser light of the moon, and the landscape became tones of silver and shadow.

"What is it?" Jill asked, as Cody knelt at the edge of the gravel bar.

"The river has stopped."

"Stopped?"

"Look."

She knelt beside him, getting a better angle of view in the moonlight. The river had fallen dramatically. Where there had been deep current, there was now only a series of dark, shallow pools, the water barely trickling from one to the next.

"So?" Jill asked.

"So that's how Riley was able to catch a fish," Cody said, pointing to where several other fish were struggling among the rocks in search of deeper water.

"No. I mean, so what does it matter if the river stops?"

Cody looked at her. "Rivers don't just stop," he said. "Especially this one."

"Why not? Maybe somebody closed the gates to a dam upstream," she suggested.

"There aren't any dams on this river," Cody said. "It's protected by law as a free-flowing stream."

"Then maybe it just ran out of water."

"Rivers don't just run out of water. It takes time and a period of drought for a stream this size to empty its watershed," Cody said.

It was obvious to Jill that he considered this an extremely abnormal event, and suddenly she had a creepy feeling that gave her goosebumps on her arms and legs.

Cody remained kneeling beside the river, as if he hoped to understand by interpretation of his own senses what had caused this to happen. Riley came up behind him and wagged his tail again. He still had the fish in his mouth and didn't know what to do with it, a problem he usually didn't have.

Cody took the fish from him, and freed of his burden, Riley took off again, racing across the wet rocks toward another group of fish that were all but left high and dry in the shallows. Cody almost stopped him but checked the impulse, and in little more than a minute, Riley was back with another fish, this one a largemouth and nearly as big as the first one.

"Well, *he* sure doesn't seem bothered that the river quit," Jill said, watching the big setter slip on the wet rocks and plow through the water on his face as he pursued a fish that doubled back between his legs.

Cody laughed, but it was a weak laugh and did not belie his concern about what had happened to the river. "Yeah, Riley likes a good thing."

The dog was back with a third fish and followed that a few minutes later with a fourth. Then he began to have trouble. The fish resumed escaping him. Fewer of them became trapped in the shallows, and it was soon apparent that the river was rising, and rising rapidly.

As Jill and Cody watched in astonishment, the river's channel filled again, and soon its current and accompanying sounds of swirling, pouring water had returned to their usual level.

"What could have caused that?" Jill asked.

"I don't know. I don't have any idea." Cody held up the last fish Riley had brought him. "But whatever it is, it gave us supper."

They watched the river a while longer, until Cody was convinced of the monotony of its routine, and then they returned to the fire. Although he didn't talk about it, Jill could tell that Cody remained deeply concerned about what had happened. Looking out into the blackness toward the river, she had another creepy feeling and a recurrence of goosebumps that made her shiver.

Cody cleaned the fish with his pocketknife and cooked them on flat stones. Even without lemon-butter, Jill thought the game fish tasted exceptional. The four large fish yielded an abundance of steaming, succulent meat, and since they were unlikely to be eating regularly for a while, Cody urged her to eat all she could now. Together, they removed the bones from what was left and gave it to Riley, who made quick work of it, licked his chops, determined that Jill was an easy mark for getting his ears rubbed and laid his big wet head in her lap.

"Thanks for dinner, Riley," she said and was conned immediately by the most elementary of his well-practiced, big-brown-loving-eyes look.

Cody was still curious about her. She was seeming less and less crazy to him, but he was still unable to reconcile her earlier, bizarre behavior. And he continued to stumble over the idea that she had been confined at Green Meadows.

"Where are you from?" he asked her.

"Center Ridge, I guess. At least that's where I live now."

"That's where I live," Cody said. "But I've never seen you before."

"My father and I just moved there last year, so I was only there for the summer. I've been attending school in St. Louis since then."

She looked up from scratching Riley's forehead. The food had improved her outlook, and she felt like talking now, especially to someone her own age. Moreover, this guy looked like a good listener. He said just enough to prompt her and get her going. Also, she began to think that he deserved to know the circumstances and events that had drawn him into a fix that for right now was as bad as her own.

"When I came home for the summer," she continued, "I thought something was wrong with my father at the time, but I couldn't tell for sure. He seemed a little remote, as if he was worried about something, but I just figured it was because he was working so hard. And then one night last week around midnight, he came tearing into the house, practically dragged me out of bed, and the next thing I knew I was in the car with him and he was driving like — like I've never *ever* seen him drive before."

"Driving where?" Cody asked.

"On the road from Center Ridge to Oak Flats. At times he was doing over a hundred."

Cody whistled. "A hundred? On *that* road?"

"More than a hundred. And then there was this light — a light in the sky. It just came out of nowhere, and then it ran ahead of us."

"What kind of a light?" Cody asked.

"I — I don't know. But it was bright, really bright, and it could move fast."

"In the sky, you mean?"

"Yes, in the sky. It just shot across the sky, and then it either went out or disappeared behind the mountain ahead of us. But a few seconds later it appeared again, and this time it was right in front of us. We were really traveling, Cody, and suddenly we couldn't see because the light was so bright. The last thing I remember is that the car was turning over and flipping off the road and I was going through the air."

"You were thrown out?" Cody asked.

"I woke up lying in vines beside the road. It was daylight, and when I looked for my father, I couldn't find him, and I couldn't find the car, either. It just wasn't there."

"Are you saying the car had disappeared?"

"I don't know what happened to it, but it was gone," she said, "just like my father, and I haven't found either of them yet." She looked at him, trying to read his reaction, but all she could tell was that he was thinking about what she said.

"Go ahead," he said. "What happened then?"

"These people came along and gave me a ride to the clinic at Oak Flats, and while I was getting my head sewed up" — she held up her hair and showed him where the stitches had been removed — "the sheriff and his deputy went back and looked for my father."

"And they didn't find him either?" Cody asked.

"No. But a little while later, they said they had reached him through Magnum Gas and that he was out in the field working, *where he had been for two days,* and he wanted me to be taken to that Green Meadows place to rest up."

"That doesn't make sense," Cody said.

"Oh really? Well, that's what I thought, too. How could he have been out working, when he was in a car wreck with me only a few hours earlier?"

"How did they explain that you had been hurt and found alongside the road?"

She shook her head. "After they had supposedly talked to my father, they weren't much concerned about that. The best the doctor could offer was that the blow to my head had messed up my thinking."

"Isn't that possible?"

"No, it isn't possible. And it isn't possible for this reason: I was in that hospital for a full week, and my father never came. Instead, Magnum Gas had someone phone every day and say that he was being detained in the field by some kind of phony emergency."

"Well? Don't oil and gas company engineers get held up by emergencies sometimes?"

"Yes," she said and then shook her head. "But if my father knew I was hurt and in a hospital, there's nothing that could stop him from coming to see about me. Nothing. I know this, Cody. *I know my father.*"

"So you ran away from the hospital?"

"That's right. I made it back to my house and got my trail bike. On the way to Oak Flats, I found the muffler that had been knocked off my father's car. I took that to the sheriff, but he wouldn't take me seriously — he just acted like I was some kind of dope who needed humoring — and when I saw that he intended to call the people at the hospital, I got out of there. I was going to Kennethville to catch a bus to the state capital, so I could get somebody to listen to me, but I ran into the police at the airport, and I was trying to hide from them when I ran into you. You know the rest."

"Who was the big guy who was trying to hold onto the plane?"

"He was the one that Magnum Gas sent to take me to the hospital in the first place. He had the nurse from the hospital with him."

Cody shook his head. It seemed like a wild, improbable story.

"You don't believe me," she said, sighing.

"I'm not sure what I believe," he said. "I might not believe the river stopped, if I hadn't seen it happen. But then I didn't see the weird light you say you saw. And I didn't see your father's car disappear into thin air. All I saw was this freaked-out girl who took me up in the sky after I had decided I didn't want to go."

Jill got tickled, thinking about it. "You should have heard yourself yelling!"

"I thought we were dead," Cody said sheepishly.

She laughed again. It was a relief to laugh, and it felt good to her. " 'You're killing me, and you have no right to kill me!' " Jill said, mimicking him good-naturedly. Then she turned quietly somber and shook her head. "I thought we were dead, too. You can't imagine how close it was. By the time we reached the river, there was nothing left that I could do. If this gravel bar hadn't been here — well, I don't think we would be here. We were lucky."

"Lucky?" Cody said, and this time they both laughed, when suddenly Riley snapped his head up from her lap.

In a flash, the setter was on his feet, the hair standing up along his spine. He growled and whimpered nervously.

Jill and Cody looked at each other, and then they seemed to hear it and feel it at the same time. A rumbling. The earth began to shake. A deep resonance shuddered up, passing through them. It came again and again, repeatedly. Then, as suddenly as it had begun, it stopped.

"What on earth was that?" Jill exclaimed. "An earthquake?"

Cody shook his head. "I don't know."

"Look!" Jill gasped, pointing.

From out of the river was rising a glimmering stream of light particles. Like metallic bits of dust, they flowed upward, bubbling from the surface of the water and collecting by the tens of thousands to form a wavering, shining cloud a few feet above the river.

Its light intensifying, the cloud ballooned to the size of a room. Then, its edges rolling under and up into its interior, it lifted into the sky.

Trees lit with its luminescence and seemed to wilt from its brilliance. The light streaked across the sky, diminishing in the distance, and then it locked itself rigidly above the horizon less than half a mile away.

"Is that the light you saw?" Cody asked.

"No," Jill replied. "I've never seen anything like that!"

# 13.

THE LIGHT REMAINED THROUGHOUT THE NIGHT AND WAS out of sight only when they closed their eyes for brief moments of rest.

They could not speculate about what it could be, because neither of them knew of any logic that could explain it.

Its undulating, wavering movements gave it an appearance of something living, and its intensity and color gave it an aura of supernatural power that would have panicked an entire population of people, had it settled over the town square rather than the middle of a wilderness.

Yet it had made no hostile move toward Cody and Jill, and in spite of its awesome presence, they experienced more wonder than fear. After talking so much that they felt they had known each other for years rather than hours, they were still alert at dawn, when the light cloud began to shift its position.

As the sky in the background became increasingly lighter, the cloud shrank, collapsing in on itself and concentrating its light as if compensating for the diminishing contrast. Then, white with brilliance, it slid slowly from the horizon and dipped into the sea of trees, its rays emanating out from their crowns like fingers from a hand.

Cody made a bearing on its position, mentally drawing a line from midpoint between the two peaks behind it to the place where they stood now, which he could recognize by the contour of the river. A few moments later, the distinct rays from the light faded, then disappeared.

Cody and Jill turned and looked at each other, communicating thoughts of mystery and disbelief.

"Listen," Cody said hesitantly, "I know you're in a hurry to get started, but there are some really strange things going on out here —"

"Yeah," Jill agreed, "and 'strange' is an understatement."

"You could go ahead and follow the river downstream, while I try to find out what the light was," he suggested. "It shouldn't take longer than a couple or three hours for me to get over there and back. Then, I could catch up with you."

She shook her head. "Uh-uh. I'm not going anywhere by myself — not now, not after all this weird stuff. No thanks. I'll stay with you."

"You don't mind?"

"Two or three hours isn't going to make all that much difference if it's going to take us two weeks to get out of here. Anyway, I'm still hoping there'll be planes out looking for us. They may as well find us here as farther downriver."

"Then let's go," Cody said.

Buoyed by his recent success at fish catching, Riley had to be told twice to get out of the water and follow them. He came unhappily, leaving the river with great reluctance, but within a few minutes, he was scouting through the woods ahead of them; and with only slightly less enthusiasm than he had for chasing fish, he now began to pursue lizards. In the early morning, even the blue-striped race runners were fairly easy to catch, and Riley thought they made excellent snacks. They were plump, and he liked the way they squirmed in his mouth. He ate several.

The terrain sloped upward away from the river, and the initial going was easy. Giant hardwoods predominated, holding the second growth in check, but higher up the mountain, enough light filtered through to support saplings and vines, and with the undergrowth came patches of sawbriar.

They walked around it when they could, but usually they were forced to pick their way through the tangles of needle-sharp thorns, with Riley carefully tiptoeing in their steps, content to allow the people to blaze the trail.

"I don't know about you, Riley," Jill said, as the dog waited patiently behind her while she disengaged her T-shirt from a runner of briar.

Cody laughed. "He's very careful about not exposing himself to any unnecessary discomfort. He doesn't like things that stick or bite."

"Well, that's understandable," Jill said. "Neither do I."

But she wasn't squeamish, Cody noticed. And she was as agile as a cat, keeping up with him easily. He had hoped that she would come with him, rather than going downriver. He had an uncomfortable feeling about these strange happenings, and he was glad there was someone to share the experience.

As for Jill, she had no choice. That they were here at all was her fault, and she had recognized much earlier that the best way to get back to civilization was to follow Cody's lead. Making do in this wilderness was second nature to him. Moreover, she liked him, especially his practical outlook and quiet air of confidence. For the first time lately, someone was on her side.

He stopped and she walked into him, the jolt interrupting her thoughts and making her oddly aware that she was glad she couldn't see what her hair looked like.

They were in an open spot, where they could look down to the river. Cody pointed in the direction from which they had come and indicated the line they were following.

"Straight ahead," he said, "about two hundred yards more. That'll be where it was when we saw it go out."

They proceeded cautiously, apprehensively. Only Riley continued on without apparent concern. He wandered along haphazardly, tracking a rabbit for a while, eating a few more lizards, and sticking his head into holes so he could snort dirt and rotting vegetation.

Ahead was a small draw, a thin slice taken out of the side of the mountain by Mesozoic erosion. The draw was thickly wooded, and they entered it at an angle, staying as close as possible to Cody's heading. Nearing its upper end, Cody stopped again.

"Look!" he said, pointing.

At the bottom of the draw, obscured by leaves and foliage, was a silver-gray color that was out of place among the dominant hues of green and brown. Exchanging looks of apprehension, they started down cautiously for a closer look.

Cody parted the sweet gum saplings at the bottom and stopped again, suddenly.

"It's a car!"

Jill stepped beside him. Her heart leaped up into her throat. "It's my father's car! Oh no!" She put her hands to her head. "My father!"

"Wait!" he said, catching her arm as she started forward on trembling legs. "Are you sure?"

Jill nodded. "Yes. I'm sure!"

"Then let me look first."

Cody approached the car not knowing what he would find. The European automobile was partially buried in the soft earth and smashed nearly beyond recognition. He made his way around to the driver's side and looked in, prepared for the worst.

# 14.

Cody glanced back at Jill and saw the anguish and dread on her face. He hurried, trying to spare her as much of the awful waiting as he could.

The car looked as if it had impacted into the ground nose first, then fallen over. The driver's side and the roof were crushed, badly compromising the survivability of anyone unfortunate enough to have been in it.

On his knees, Cody looked inside the car, then under it. Standing, he shook his head.

"No one."

Jill hurried to the car and got down on her knees beside it to look inside. She was shocked by the extent of damage and sickened by the idea that her father could have been in it. On the back rest of the driver's seat was a dried stain, and she had another bad moment of apprehension when she realized what it was.

"Blood!" she exclaimed fearfully.

"But it's not very much blood," Cody countered. "A cut

that was only minor could bleed that much easily — especially in warm weather like this."

Jill saw an object lying on the torn headliner and pulled it out. "My purse!" she said, opening it and drawing out her driver's license and private pilot's license for him to see. "You have to believe me now!"

Cody looked at her and said seriously, "I had already made up my mind to believe you — everything you said. But if I had any doubts, this sure erases them."

"If we're where you say we are and there aren't any roads, how can my father's car be here?" she asked. "How could the car end up out in the middle of nowhere?"

Cody shook his head. "I don't know, but there's a logical explanation for everything. Maybe the light had something to do with it."

"Which light? The one that caused the wreck in the first place, or the one we saw last night? They weren't the same. And what's the explanation for the lights? I'm not sure that I see any logic in anything!"

Cody pointed to an overhead limb that was broken, hanging by the strength of its bark. "It looks to me like the car was just dropped in here, and it had to have been several days ago for the leaves on that limb to have dried and turned brown like that. So the light we saw couldn't have had anything to do with it — at least not last night anyway."

"A lot of strange things are happening here, if you ask me."

"Such as?" Cody asked.

"Such as the fact that we ran out of gas in the plane and were forced down into the one spot within fifty miles that wouldn't kill us. Only we didn't really run out of gas. The fuel line just clogged."

"That's not so hard to believe. Things like that can happen."

"Except that it happened here — right here," Jill said. "Right by a place where this strange, freaky light appears!" She shook her head in disbelief. "I'm beginning to think that maybe all those people were right. Maybe I *am* crazy. Maybe I'm imagining all this!"

"Well, if you're imagining it, then I'm imagining it, too. And if you're crazy, then I'm crazy, too, and that's another couple of coincidences. No, there's a logical explanation for everything — even this."

"Well, it bothers me, Cody," Jill replied. "It just *bothers* me."

Cody shook his head, thinking. "There's a logical explanation for everything."

Riley came down the side of the draw after having given up a halfhearted start on the trail of a rabbit. He was panting and hot. He sniffed the car once or twice with only a little interest, then lay down beside it, trying to get against the cool earth. He had seen cars everywhere else, so he didn't think it strange to find one here, too.

"So what do we do now?" Jill asked, looking at Cody in bewilderment.

"We could get started downstream," he suggested, "and try to get the sheriff or somebody out here as soon as possible. If we really push ourselves, we might be able to make it in nine or ten days. Or — or we could head upstream."

"Upstream?" she asked, and then she quickly caught on, saying, "Because all these weird things might be related —"

"The light, the rumbling last night, and —"

"And the river stopping!" she said. "Whatever stopped the river would have had to have stopped it upstream."

Cody nodded. "But we don't know how far upstream. It could take longer going that way than going downstream for help. And we might not find anything."

But their decisions were already made. Neither would be able to leave here without at least making an effort to follow up on what seemed to be an incredible series of events, logical or otherwise.

The revelation of the wrecked car was the ultimate drawing card for Jill. She could not just tuck that away into a corner of her mind for the length of time it would take to reach the authorities and convince them to come out here.

Together, they searched outward from where they found the car, making an ever-increasing circle, until they were convinced there was nothing else extraordinary in the vicinity.

Stopping occasionally to pick and eat berries, they made their way back to the river and began the trek of unknown distance upstream. The dense growth along the banks made it more practical to use the river channel itself as their path. Whenever possible, they waded through the shallows at its edges, but at times they were forced to swim and frequently had to struggle against the current of the numerous rapids.

There were advantages to following the river. Serious trouble from insects, particularly chiggers and ticks, was avoided, and the clear, tumbling water of the Patawa was a pleasant contrast to the increasing heat of the summer day.

Riley, whose long red coat made him suffer most from the heat, thought the outing had turned into something grand. He pursued fish with abandon, catching none.

It was hunger that made them stop while there were still a few hours left in the day. Arriving at a wide, rocky area of the river containing several small, shallow pools, Cody suggested that Jill start a fire while he tried his skill at spearing fish with a sharpened stick.

Riley intended to help, but the first fish he tried to ambush was also the one his master was standing motionless and poised in wait of, and the reward for his enthusiastic, and unsuccessful, attack was to be ordered from the river and made to stay with Jill. How soon they had forgotten how well he had provided for them the night before.

Without Riley in his way, Cody had good success. He speared several rock bass and bream, and by the time he got them cleaned, Jill had the fire going.

"Nice," Cody said, watching the fire as tongues of flame began to lick upward through the dry kindling she had gathered and arranged with the kind of precision that he admired. "I'd say we're almost ready to eat."

"I went to a summer camp when I was nine," Jill said. "The only thing I learned was how to build a fire, but I never forgot it. I dropped a couple of good pieces of wood down by the water. After I put those on, I think the fire will do okay."

She turned to go after the wood, but Cody stopped her.

"Let Riley do a little work."

She looked at him quizically.

"Riley," he said sharply, and when the setter looked at

107

him, Cody moved his arm out in a high arc, pointing away from where he stood toward the river, where two sticks of bleached driftwood the size of baseball bats lay on the gravel shore.

Immediately Riley began moving in that direction. When he hesitated, Cody repeated the signal, and he headed that way with more assurance that that was indeed what he was supposed to do. When he reached the pieces of wood, Cody extended his arm straight overhead, and the red dog stopped, then stood watching him.

Now Cody clasped both hands together, in the signal between them that meant pick-it-up, and Riley looked around, wondering what to get. He hesitated, but the sticks of wood were so obvious he couldn't miss them. He picked one up. It had a pleasant texture and was no trouble for his big jaws, so he didn't mind at all. After the next signal from his master, he returned at a half trot and dropped the piece of wood at Cody's feet.

"I think I'm impressed," Jill said.

Cody shook his head. "You shouldn't be. He's capable of doing better than that, but I haven't worked with him very much lately, so he's not as sharp as he can be.

"In fact, he's gotten downright sloppy," he added a few moments later, after sending Riley back for the remaining piece of wood, only to have him walk past it to sniff curiously at a wet spot left by a tiny green frog.

"Riley!" he said sternly, and the setter returned to business, albeit somewhat reluctantly.

"That's still pretty good," Jill said after Riley had dropped the piece of wood at his master's feet again.

Cody talked scornfully to his dog but laughed and rubbed his floppy ears, too. "You can never tell for sure about this hound. Sometimes he does great. And sometimes he does a whole lot less than great — it all depends on how life strikes him at the time. But he's rusty right now, and that's mostly my fault for neglecting his lessons. When we get back home, I'm going to change that, do you hear, Riley?"

Riley thumped his tail, unconcerned.

They ate their fill of fish simmered on flat stones and flavored with the tender, mild shoots of wild onions, and again there was enough left over for Riley.

As the day faded, they sat on a patch of moss-covered bank and savored the moment of full stomachs and rest. Jill worked the comb she had taken from her purse through her wet, tangled hair. She had hoped they would find something else today, perhaps a clue to help unravel the mysterious goings-on, but she did not feel unduly disappointed that they hadn't. More than anything else, she felt pleasantly surprised that they had been doing so well. She was tired but not drained of strength, and right now, she wasn't even hungry.

"You're pretty good with that spear," she said.

Cody laughed. "I think before we're through, all three of us are going to be tired of fish."

"Did Joe Tiotec teach you how to do that?"

"No, not really. I taught myself mostly. But he was the reason I tried it. He told me the Patawa Indians speared fish by standing on rocks and being careful not to cast a shadow over the water. It's really not so hard. You just have to be real still and learn that water bends light rays, so the fish aren't where they appear to be."

Previous inquiries concerning how he acquired so many river skills and so much knowledge about the Preservation Area had invariably brought up Joe Tiotec's name, and Jill rapidly realized how deeply Cody had been influenced by his Indian-anthropologist friend. "How did you get to know Joe Tiotec?" she asked, curious to know more.

"Like this," Cody said, gesturing with his open hands and remembering with fond sadness. "As soon as I was old enough, I started floating the Patawa. Me and Riley. We kept running into Joe out here, and after a while we got to be friends. He had been studying the Patawa Indians most of his life, and by the time I met him, he was already an old man. His eyesight was getting bad, too, but he knew this river and the country around it so well he hardly even needed eyes anyway."

"And you started working with him," Jill said, prompting him to continue.

"It just sort of happened," Cody said. "There were a lot of things I could do to help out — like lifting things and paddling the canoe. And Joe knew so much!" Cody's voice took on a tone of quiet enthusiasm, and he looked directly at her, wanting her to know what she could never truly know without having known Joe Tiotec herself. "I mean, he fascinated me! I felt honored that he would even consent to have me around!

"Listen," he continued, and Jill could see the spark in his eyes, "we excavated a portion of a thousand-year-old Patawa village site about fifteen miles upriver from here. Just Joe and me — and Riley. We dug inch by inch, layer by layer, digging into the lives of those people, digging into their habits

110

and secrets, finding out things about them that no one would ever have known otherwise. I know that might not sound interesting, digging up the ground for bits of pottery or bone or sifting through the ash of some ancient fire, but Joe Tiotec made it one of the most exciting experiences of my life! That's the kind of a man he was!"

"What kind of people were the Patawa Indians?" Jill asked.

Immediately Cody opened that well-documented mental file and skimmed the highlights. "They were hunter-gatherers," he said. "Peaceful — in a study that covered more than two thousand years of their history, Joe was never able to find any evidence of collective violence, like war or human sacrifice. They had a high sense of social order, yet everyone was so equal in political stature that it was truly an egalitarian democracy.

"And they were artists and craftsmen. There are paintings and etchings on stone and walls of caves in these hills that are so good and so detailed you feel funny if you refer to them as primitive. The Patawas dug clay from the banks of the river and made pottery and sculptures, which they fired to nearly two thousand degrees in coal-burning kilns. That was a real technological accomplishment."

"Why haven't I heard of these people before now?" Jill asked.

"Well, they were isolated," Cody said, "almost completely. And there were never very many of them. At their most populous, there were probably no more than five to seven thousand of them living in about a half dozen villages all up and down the Patawa River Valley."

"Did they live in teepees?"

"No. They built houses of rock and wattle and daub. Some of them had several rooms."

"What's wattle and daub?"

"Sticks and mud — or in this case, clay, from the Patawa River.

"They were a happy, cheerful people who loved their family and friends and shared a strong sense of community," Cody continued, borrowing one of the summary sentences he remembered from helping proofread Joe Tiotec's papers. "And they believed the Patawa River and the surrounding country represented the best of all possible worlds. It never failed to provide for them — just like the river has given us fish. They considered it holy." Cody made a sweeping motion with his arms. "The mountains and everything. All of it!"

"What happened to the Patawas?" she asked.

"Civilization," Cody replied. "Finally, it got too close and began to draw them away, especially the young people, and in a little while there was hardly anyone left."

"And Joe Tiotec was the last," she said.

"Yes. The very last."

Jill saw the misty look in Cody's eyes, and it gave her a good feeling to know someone who could feel the way he did. "But just think," she said. "Because Joe Tiotec was an anthropologist and studied the Patawas so extensively, in a way, he did what no one else could have done. He enabled them to live forever."

"That's right!" Cody said, liking that thought very much. "He did, didn't he."

"And from what you've told me about him, I think he

would be happy to know that you scattered his ashes in the river," Jill said. "I think that was an appropriate thing to do — sort of like returning his spirit to where it began."

They let the fire go out, and as night fell, they leaned back on the mossy bank, propped their heads in their hands, and continued talking.

Jill told Cody how her father's job had caused them to move around a lot and how, as a result, she had usually gone to private schools. She told him about going to school in St. Louis, which was okay but something less than fantastic, and he told her about going to school in Center Ridge, which also wasn't fantastic, but wasn't so bad either.

Riley had no complaints.

The setter's lips quivered in a long, contented sigh and under the gentle touch of Jill's hand he began drifting toward sleep. Then, without knowing why, without there being time to know anything, he was suddenly alert. And upset.

He whined, turned a quick circle and whimpered, then whined again.

A moment later, Jill and Cody heard what Riley heard, a crackling sound, followed by a long, high-pitched hiss. The hiss grew louder and louder, until it seemed it would split the night air. Then it began to fade away, like a tire with its air exhausted, rising briefly in a final rush before dying completely.

Jill and Cody looked at each other. Riley whimpered.

For nearly an hour, the rippling surface of the river had sparkled with soft points of moon- and starlight, but suddenly it drew their attention with a more dazzling display. The dots and wavering slashes of silver began to boil, increasing in

113

number and becoming a swirl of colors that rose out of the water as a small, glowing nebula. Hanging a few feet above the river, the cloud rolled in on itself and wavered, then began moving slowly upstream.

"Uh-oh!" Jill said. "Here we go again!"

The light cloud moved upstream about two hundred feet, and then, as they watched it, it either went out or disappeared. As soon as it was gone, they heard something else, but this time it was the unmistakable whop-whop of a helicopter, a big one.

The chopper came in low, following the river, making willows dance in the wash of its big rotor as it passed overhead. The powerful searchlight between its skids spotted its path and made everything it touched seem to withdraw from its searing whiteness. As quickly as it had come, it was gone, disappearing behind the next ridge.

"That's the light I saw!" Jill exclaimed. "That's the one that caused us to wreck! I couldn't hear that it was a helicopter because we were on a gravel road and the muffler was knocked off and the windows were rolled up!"

"It could carry a car easily," Cody said. "And drop it in the middle of nowhere."

"Magnum Gas!" Jill said. "They have helicopters. It's how they move their field camps around!"

# 15.

BOTH FELT A SENSE OF URGENCY, AND THEY PUSHED THEM-
selves. This was not the time to reflect on the beauty of the
river or the pleasantness of its water. Instead, the river was an
obstacle — less formidable than the surrounding woods but
an obstacle nonetheless.

It had to be negotiated, waded, swum. Its rocks had to be
climbed upon and over.

Riley didn't like it. Each time he got interested in something, he found himself being left behind, and being left behind was perhaps his greatest fear in life.

Sometimes he was left behind when Cody went to school.
A few times he had been left behind at the veterinarian's,
where awful things were done to him. Once, he jumped out
of the back of the truck at a stoplight because he saw a squir-
rel run up a tree, and he had been left behind in an area
where he had never been before. He had wandered around
for two days with nothing to eat before Cody finally found
him.

Now he had to pay attention so something like that wouldn't happen to him again.

Cody wondered about their pace. They were covering ground (and water) fast enough that he felt the strain. But Jill kept up, and she didn't complain, and he continued to be more than a little amazed by her.

Not only was she able to slog through mud, scramble over rocks and swim deep holes fully clothed as well as he could, she also managed to look good doing it. They were both continually wet, their jeans and shirts sticking to them, and he had little doubt as to which of them looked better that way.

Once she got her hair combed out, Jill fixed it behind her and out of the way in a ponytail. Her compact mirror had been shattered in the wreck of her father's car, and she had no idea how her hair looked. Being overly concerned with her appearance did not fit in the current situation, but she did wonder about it. A pimple could have grown on her face by now and she wouldn't have even known it was there. She was definitely uncomfortable with the idea that when Cody looked at her he might be seeing a big zit.

By noon, they were both hungry, but in silent consent, they continued to push on, slowing only to pick a handful of berries at the river's edge and to tear off and chew the bitter leaves of a poke sallet plant.

By midafternoon, with the day at its hottest, they were beginning to feel the wear. Cody was considering calling a rest, when it happened again — the hissing noise.

This time it was louder and lasted longer before fading out, and a few minutes later it came again, a high hissing noise that died away like the end of a sigh.

"It sounds close!" Cody said. "Which way do you think?"

Jill pointed on a line that went up the side of a ridge that was almost perpendicular to the river. "There."

Cody agreed. "That's what it sounded like to me. What do you say we do?" He looked at her, and she nodded.

"Suppose it's something that's hungry?" he asked.

"Don't say that. It's not funny. Remember, you said there's a logical explanation for everything."

"Yes, but I'm still in my formative years. I'm subject to having my mind changed."

"Cute," she said, giving him a shove. "Let's go."

They left the river and began climbing, angling up through the dense growth and working toward the ridge in the direction from which they had heard the hiss.

Compared to the mountainside, the river now seemed like a highway. The sides of the low mountain formations were thick with underbrush and sawbriar, and the heated afternoon air was so saturated with humidity that it was like trying to breathe through a blanket. Now, too, gnats and biting flies buzzed about their faces, making their land hike a lesson in misery.

The farther they went from the river, the less sure they became of the correct direction. They might have gone off course entirely, but the noise came again, so loud this time it was more blast than hiss.

"There!" Jill said, pointing through the trees and underbrush on the side of the slope a short distance ahead. "And I think I saw something move!"

The noise rose again and died back, but this time it did not stop completely. A low, soft hiss remained, and they

made their way toward it with a familiar feeling of apprehension.

"Listen," Jill said, catching Cody's arm and stopping him.
"What if you're right? What if it *is* hungry?"

"Then maybe it'll eat Riley first," Cody said, which was
unlikely, because Riley was staying well behind them.

However, the closer they came to the source, the less likely
it seemed that the noise was being made by something living.
In addition, Riley wasn't alarmed by it. What was bothering
him was the heat. He couldn't understand why anyone
would leave the coolness of the river to come up into this hot
mountain jungle.

They saw it ahead of them, a flash of something white that
came with an increase in the level of the sound.

"Steam!" Cody said. "It's a blast of steam!"

They came out into an area about the size of a room. It
had been cleared of trees but was well overgrown with weeds,
seedlings, and sawbriar. At its center protruded the mouth of
a badly corroded steel pipe, about a foot in diameter. Like ex-
haust from a rocket, a column of steam shot from the pipe
and was swallowed up by the sweltering, humid air, the
plume disappearing only a little above the height of the surrounding trees.

The air smelled of burned stuff, of hot rocks and minerals,
and it was sulfurous. A crackling sound came out of the pipe
and the volume of steam increased suddenly, blasting into the
sky and producing the hissing noise, so loud at this proximity
that they both clapped their hands to their ears.

"Wow!" Jill said, after it had died down again. "What's
the deal with that thing?"

118

Cody shook his head. "I don't know. Maybe it's some kind of geothermal activity, but I've never heard of there being any around here."

"Well, the pipe didn't grow. Somebody put it there."

"Yeah — and I wonder why. It doesn't look like there's anything else nearby, but we better check to make sure."

There wasn't. They made a wide circle through the woods around the clearing, and the only results of their search were expended energy and its consequent effects on their level of fatigue, several more scratches from sawbriar, and, for Jill, a spot on the back of her hand that slowly spread out into hundreds of tiny seed ticks, each of which had to be dealt with before it had a chance to locate its lunch.

"Except for the fact that there's something hot down there, we don't know much more than we did," Cody said.

"At least we know it's not something alive," Jill replied. "I don't know about you, but that makes me feel a lot better."

"It also supports my basic premise, that there's a logical explanation for everything — unless, of course, the steam is caused by the snoring of a fire-breathing dragon," Cody added with a tone of cleverness that made Jill groan.

They watched the steam for a few minutes longer. There was nothing regular about its eruptions, and there was no water being blown out ahead of it — only the scalding hot vapor, whose source of heat remained a mystery.

They made their way back to the river and welcomed the relief of its water. Riley was especially grateful to be out of the woods. He had been afraid they were going to stay there.

The river gave them a feeling of refreshment, and they continued upstream, trudging through the shallows and avoiding the current and deeper water as much as possible. But they were already tired and hungry, and over the ensuing hours, they grew more tired and more hungry.

The previously open banks began to rise more steeply, channeling the river into deep, slow-moving stretches of water. With less than an hour of daylight remaining, they found themselves between rock and earthen walls that were nearly as steep and high as a canyon's and facing more than three hundred yards of dead, flat river as their next obstacle.

Jill looked at the oceanic expanse of water and groaned. "I don't know about that," she said.

"We've got to have something to eat," Cody said. "That means fish."

"Great!" she replied, spotting a flat place against one side that looked just right for a person to lie down. "We can stop right here, and you can go stick us some fish."

Cody shook his head. "I can't get any fish here. It's too deep. I need shallows, with lots of rocks sticking up that I can stand on." Jill had already started for the place she had picked out to lie down, but he stopped her. "Come on. There's a good area above here, at the top of the next rapids. We can swim it in ten or fifteen minutes, and there'll still be time for me to get us a couple of fish."

Jill groaned again. "Aren't you tired?"

"Yes, of course I'm tired. I'm as tired as you are, but if we're going to eat, we're going to have to swim."

"I think maybe I'm more tired than I am hungry," she said.

"We need to eat," he insisted, and she knew he was right.

Wading into deeper water, they lay out and began the slow, steady side-stroking that they had used to swim other long holes of water and that seemed best suited to lessen the handicap of wearing shoes.

Riley quickly outdistanced them and made circles, scouting ahead for something interesting among the willows growing out of the walls on each side. He was hungry, and he thought if he looked he might find something to eat.

Swimming side by side, Cody and Jill had covered nearly half the distance, when the progress that Jill had been measuring stroke by stroke against the side seemed suddenly to stop.

"Why aren't we getting anywhere?" she asked, frustrated. "I thought there wasn't supposed to be any current out here."

Cody rolled over on his other side. She was right. Not only had their progress stopped, but they seemed to be losing ground they had already gained.

"What is it? What's happening?" Jill asked, concerned now.

Cody rolled over again, looking, getting as high in the water as he could. They were moving with the current now and rapidly gaining speed. In addition, the level of the river was falling again — but much faster than he had seen it happen before.

Astonished, the two of them watched the level of the water plummet at the sides of the river, and then a deep sucking noise tore through the air.

The arched top of a tunnel appeared in the side of the river nearest them, and the gaping hole grew ever larger as the falling water level uncovered its full dimensions.

Rushing into the tunnel, the river's entire volume rammed against itself, swirling and leaping crazily.

"Swim!" Cody shouted.

Jill was already swimming. They both reached desperately for water, kicking frantically. In their panic, they gained against the current, but it was only for the briefest of moments, and then their efforts were useless.

They were hardly more than matchsticks in the incredible rush of water. Its sudden power so shocked their senses that neither of them had even the presence of mind to shout out their horror or indignation. In the last instant before they were swept into the gaping maw of the tunnel, they barely managed to reach out and grasp each other's hand, and then they were gone.

*   *   *

Only Riley was able to keep from going down the hole that suddenly opened in the side of the river. From farther upstream, he saw Jill and Cody disappear, and he knew immediately he didn't want to go where they went.

With webbed feet that were characteristic of his breed, he was a powerful swimmer, and he swam now as he had never swum before.

His chest nearly leaped from the water as he drove his legs in full-bore, scared-crazy desperation. He gave it everything he had.

He held against the current, and he continued to hold against the current, until the river was so low that his feet struck bottom. Then he waded, until he was in water shallow enough for him to run.

And then he ran.

# 16.

Jill thought of her father. She was afraid she was going to die without ever knowing what happened to him. It didn't seem right, or fair. But if he was already dead himself, then perhaps she was on her way to another dimension right now to join him. As she was swept toward what she perceived as the certainty of her own death, she found that thought strangely comforting.

Cody had a recurrence of the feeling he had experienced several times in the past two days — that none of this was really happening. There was no such thing as a cavernous hole in the side of the river's channel. He knew the Patawa, and he knew better. Holes to suck them away like a pair of bugs down a drain did not exist.

But this one obviously *did* exist, and the force of the water rushing through it was absolute. They could do nothing. Struggling was useless. Indeed, there was nothing to struggle for. There were only darkness, dankness, and the sensation of speed as they were swept along.

They awaited what they thought was inevitable — collisions that would batter them to death or violent turbulence that would pull them under and hold them there until they drowned.

But Cody was swept against the side of the tunnel, and pushing away, he realized it was unnaturally smooth. And there was something else: the tunnel also seemed perfectly straight. They had not yet experienced even the slightest bend or angle.

"Look!" Jill shouted, her voice coming back harshly from the sides of the tunnel.

A pinprick of light appeared suddenly in the darkness ahead of them. An instant later, it had grown, and in another instant they were thrust into an explosion of light.

Through churning, foaming water, they fell, pitching, rolling, finally floating upward through a froth of bubbles.

Cody surfaced first, looking for Jill, and a moment later she came up beside him. Propelled by the current, they were still moving fast. Behind them, they could see where the tunnel came out of the side of the mountain, draining away and rerouting the entire volume of the river at the command of a pair of large steel sluice gates, now standing open at each side.

Ahead of them, the onrushing water ripped through the trunks of trees, bending saplings like fishing poles and washing high up the side of an ancient river channel.

Staying together, they swam at angles with the current to avoid being slammed into the trunks of the trees. The newly filled river bent sharply and began to spread out between narrow strips of bank that gave way to bluffs towering several hundred feet on each side.

In the lessening current, Cody and Jill angled for the nearest bank. They swam through the tops of submerged willows, then waded through flooded undergrowth to dry ground, where, at last, they stood, dripping wet and exhausted.

"Are you okay?" Cody asked.

"No, I'm not okay," she replied. "And I may not ever be okay again!"

"I mean are you hurt?"

Jill shook her head. "I don't think so. Where are we?"

"I'm not sure," Cody said. "It looks like somebody bored through the mountain and diverted the river in another direction."

"Magnum Gas! Boring holes is their specialty!"

"But I wonder why," Cody said. "Come on. Let's see."

Walking a short distance toward the base of the bluff, they came to a narrow road that ran parallel to the flow of water and was deeply rutted from the steel tracks of heavy machinery.

"Which way?" Jill asked.

"Let's go back the way we came. I want to have a better look at that tunnel."

A walk of a few hundred feet down the road brought them to within view of the side of the mountain, where the water was continuing to rush from the gaping hole. Cody saw something move beside the left sluice gate. He grasped Jill's arm, pulling her off the edge of the road and behind a tree.

A man was standing on a catwalk at one side of the sluice

gates. One hand rested on a lever, and the other held a walkie-talkie to his ear. For a moment he listened, and then he spoke into the radio.

"Do you think he saw us?" Jill asked.

"Maybe not. The gate would have blocked his view of us coming out of the tunnel, and unless he was paying close attention, he probably missed us in all that turbulence."

The man listened again to the radio, then folded his arms and leaned back against the railing.

"He doesn't look too excited," Jill said.

"Then let's take a chance and see what's at the other end of this road," Cody replied.

Retracing their steps, they went farther, cautiously following the road around the bend.

"What about Riley?" Jill asked. "What do you think happened to him?"

Cody laughed. "It scares him to be left by himself, so I imagine he's looking for us by now. He has a pretty good nose, so he'll probably turn up sooner or later."

The predominant noise was the sound of water, rushing and swirling through the trees of the overgrown river channel, but a hundred yards beyond the bend, they began to make out another noise — a steady droning.

"Sounds like a diesel generator," Cody said.

"And I think I see something," Jill said a moment later.

At the side of the road ahead of them was a visible break in the tree line, and a large, rounded object protruded outward.

"Let's get off the road," Cody said.

Tediously picking their way through the underbrush and

126

ever-present sawbriar, they approached a clearing that occupied most of the narrow bank between the side of the bluff and the edge of the water. In another minute, they had a clear view of the object, its main rotor blades plainly visible against the sky.

"The helicopter!" Jill said, and the obvious connection between it and her father's car made her heart begin to pound.

For several minutes they waited, watching, while the droning noise of the generator beyond enticed them to continue on, to see what else they might find. When finally they were convinced there was no one else around, they stepped into the clearing and ran, crossing the open area as quickly as possible and stopping in the shadow of the helicopter.

Jill placed her hand on the smooth metal skin of the fuselage. This was a big industrial helicopter, powerful, with twin turbine engines, easily adequate for carrying heavy equipment — or a wrecked car — in its sling.

Crossing to the other side of the helicopter landing zone, they entered the woods again. Below this part of the bluff, the ground became rocky with outcrops of lichen-covered boulders, which made the trees more sparse and reduced the amount of undergrowth. Because the going was considerably easier now, they moved quickly.

Cody stopped suddenly and held up his hand. Jill plowed into him and nearly knocked him down.

"Thanks," he said.

"Well, you should warn me when you stop like that. I was just trying to keep up."

Cody pointed. "Look! There's a whole operation going on!"

The forest came to an end at a point between the water

and where the road widened into a broad strip of bare, well-used ground, most of which was covered by a long run of camouflage netting that was strung upward and anchored to the bluff twenty or twenty-five feet above the ground. Lined against the base of the bluff beneath the netting were a half dozen portable buildings, some with their lights turned on inside. There were also several motorized all-terrain vehicles and a small bulldozer, which appeared to be in one of the last stages of being dismantled.

"There's where the river goes!" Cody said.

Beyond the row of cabins, the ground terminated abruptly at the edge of the old channel, and the entire flow of water was diverted into another tunnel that was several times the size of the one at the other end. Three men in hard hats stood on the ground above it, watching the river swirl and spin and roar before disappearing into the cavernous hole.

A moment later, another man stepped from the nearest building and signaled them with his hand. Immediately one of the group of men brought a two-way radio to his mouth, spoke into it, then put it against his ear to listen.

Within a minute, the flow was suddenly reduced dramatically, and within a few more minutes, it came to a complete stop, leaving behind a conspicuous silence that accentuated the steady droning of the generator.

Now the deep rumbling began, sounding at first like distant thunder, then gradually increasing, until a series of tremors began to shake the earth. A small amount of gravel and clay broke from the face of the opposite bluff and sifted downward, raining into one of the pools of water remaining in the old river channel. Then the tremors stopped, and again there was only the droning of the generator and whirring of air conditioners attached to the buildings.

The three men exchanged uneasy looks. One of them said something, and they all laughed, also uneasily. Talking among themselves, they began walking along the row of portable buildings.

"They're going to eat," Jill said.

"How can you tell?"

"My gosh, can't you smell?"

Cody had been concentrating so intensely in trying to figure out what was going on that he hadn't noticed the aroma. But now he did, and it made his mouth water.

"Real food!" Jill said. "Chicken. Vegetables."

"Mashed potatoes and gravy," Cody added.

The door opened at the end building again, and the man who had signaled for the water to be shut off came out. Turning to one side, he held the door open for a second man, who hobbled out on crutches, his left leg in a cast to the knee.

Jill was behind Cody, her hands on his shoulders. Suddenly she dug in with her fingers. "My father! That's my father!" she exclaimed, barely managing to hold her voice within the limits of a whisper. "He's alive! He's alive!" she said joyously, shaking Cody so hard it rattled his vision. "I knew they had him!"

"They're going to have us too, if you don't be quiet!" Cody said, giving her a little shake of her own.

The three men were coming closer, apparently to pass within a few feet of where they were hiding. Jill and Cody dropped to the ground, kneeling beside each other in sweet-gum seedlings.

As the men approached, Jill saw the revolver strapped high on the hip of the biggest man, and a second later, she realized that he was the same man who had chased her at the airport and driven the limousine that had taken her to Green Meadows.

*   *   *

For a while, Riley had been afraid, and then the fear wore off, and he got upset. He whined and whimpered a lot, because sometimes when he did that, Cody came and told him to shut up. He usually didn't like being told to shut up, but it would be all right now if whining would make Cody suddenly appear and say that to him.

But Cody didn't appear, and Riley realized that what he feared most in life had happened — he had been left behind. The two people had gone off (it no longer seemed important that they had been sucked against their will down a hole), and they had left him behind.

Driven by a kind of restless despair, he started moving. So disturbed was he that he even left the river channel and followed his odd mix of instincts, climbing until he was as high as he could go and then going down again.

A scent came on the late-afternoon breeze, and it excited him immediately. The scent was his master's. And there was also the nice smell of the girl who would rub his ears so long.

Trotting, Riley followed his nose. He went through a patch of sawbriar without consideration for hair or hide, and when he reached the road he started running. His master's scent was stronger than ever, and the anticipation was making him happy.

Riley saw a figure walking in the growing darkness ahead, and he rushed it. The figure wheeled around suddenly, and Riley stopped.

Instinctively, the man had started to defend himself with the antennae of his walkie-talkie, but now he saw it was only a dog.

"Hello, poochie," he said and looked around suspiciously.

The man held his hand out, and Riley went to him. The hand rubbed his ears, and it felt good, but it wasn't the hand he was looking for. Pulling away, Riley ran again.

The scent was strong now and rapidly becoming stronger. Riley had no doubt that soon he would no longer be in a state of having been left behind.

He saw people ahead, and he raced toward them. The scents of his master and the girl were everywhere.

The three men jumped back in surprise when the big dark animal came frisking in among them, and then they saw what it was, only a dog rushing from hand to hand, nuzzling them in a kind of crazy affection.

"Where did he come from?" one man asked, and the big man's hand went to his revolver.

He still didn't have the right hand, Riley realized. But it was here somewhere! He knew it was!

There! The scent was so strong and so familiar it snatched his head to one side. Whimpering and whining, yelping with joy, he dived in among the sweetgum seedlings, wallowing in worshipful love all over his master.

"Up! Out of there!" ordered the man with the gun.

Cody and Jill came up slowly from their hiding place. Riley continued to jump at his master, nuzzling him and whining with joy.

Cody just looked at him and shook his head slowly. "Way to go, Riley."

Riley sat back and thumped his tail in exuberance.

Her expression fixed in anger, Jill stepped toward the man holding the gun and demanded, "I want to see my father!"

# 17.

Jill threw herself into her father's arms and began to cry with relief. Cody watched the joyful reunion and thought about his own parents. They would be worried sick, wondering what could have happened to him.

"I was afraid you were dead!" Jill said, trying to stop crying, only to become choked with thick sobs. "I — I didn't know what I would do!"

Nathan Faraday crushed his daughter's thick hair to her temples and held her head between his hands, wiping the tears from her cheeks with his thumbs.

Then the geologist's tender expression changed to anger. Turning, he said, "At least have the courtesy to leave us alone!"

The big man with the gun shrugged, then turned and walked out of the small metal building. Cody watched the door swing to and heard the shackle come together and the heavy padlock snap closed on the other side.

"Daddy, this is Cody Burke," Jill said. "A friend." She

looked at Cody and amplified her statement. "A really good friend. I keep trying to get us into trouble, and he keeps trying to get us out. He's kind and patient and clever and smart and —" She looked at Cody again and smiled, and he felt his ears beginning to burn. "Actually, what he is is terrific! Cody, this is my father. He's terrific, too."

Nathan Faraday laughed and extended a firm, warm handshake. "After an introduction like that, Cody, I feel obligated to say that I'm honored."

Cody stammered with embarrassment, but managed to say, "It's a pleasure to meet you, sir."

"Daddy, how bad is your leg?"

"Not so bad," he said. "It's fractured but not compound."

"We found your car where they dropped it. There was blood in it."

Her father turned his head, showing her the cut behind his ear. It was almost healed. "It wasn't serious, but I was knocked out. You, too, they told me. They didn't see you get thrown from the car and couldn't find you, so they weren't sure you were with me. When I came to, I started hollering about it. I was afraid you were lying dead beside the road. Then they located you and arranged to have you hospitalized. That's where I thought you were now. How did you end up here?"

Jill looked at Cody, shook her head, and sighed. "It's a long story."

Nathan Faraday hobbled painfully to a chair in the corner opposite the bunk beds and sat down, elevating his broken leg on a footstool stacked with pillows. "So tell me about it. I've got time to listen."

Starting at the moment of the car wreck, Jill began to bring him up to date. "They tried to make it look like I was crazy. The doctor and the sheriff at Oak Flats said Magnum Gas hooked them up to you by radio and that they talked to you while you were out in the field, where you had supposedly been at the time the helicopter was running us off the road."

Her father nodded. "I'm sure they did talk to someone, but it was somebody at the company playing the part. It sure wasn't me."

"But why would they go to all the trouble?"

"Because you were already in the hands of the authorities. They couldn't just kidnap you, so they arranged something slick instead. It was easy enough for them to do."

"But why?"

"To assure my cooperation. As long as they had you in their control, they knew I would do whatever they wanted."

"What is that, Daddy? What *do* they want with you?"

"To help them commit larceny. Grand larceny." He shook his head, thinking about it. "In fact, you might call it the *grandest* larceny, because its scale is almost unimaginable. But you still haven't told me how you ended up out here."

"I guess it was just stupid luck, or coincidence, or fate — or something." She looked at Cody.

"It just seemed to *happen*," he said, agreeing.

Jill related the remaining incidents of escaping from the hospital, fleeing into the crowd at the airport, and eventually ending up in the plane with Cody and Riley in the rear cockpit. "Then the engine quit, and we went in — just downriver from here."

135

"You put the Stearman down out *here* — and walked away from it?" her father asked incredulously.

"It didn't look like it, but there was just enough room to keep from killing us," Cody said. "The plane went all the way up under the trees. It used every inch of space. If we had come in from any other direction, or even if the angle had been just a little different, we never would have made it. She did a great job."

"I didn't do anything," Jill countered quickly. "Like I said, it was blind luck."

"And something of a coincidence that it happened so close to here," her father added.

"Then a lot of strange things started happening — like the river stopping and the ground shaking and rumbling . . ."

"And this strange light, Dr. Faraday," Cody said. "It came up out of the river, kind of bubbled up and formed a glowing cloud —"

"And then we found your car. That was yesterday," Jill said. "And then last night we saw the helicopter, and this afternoon we got sucked in here with the rest of the river when they let the water in."

Jill's father looked at them in astonishment and then shook his head. "Well, it's all certainly unfortunate. If I had known you had gotten away, or if only you *had* been able to reach the FBI, then maybe we could have stopped" — he turned his palms up in a gesture of defeat — "maybe we could have stopped this."

"What is it, Daddy? What's going on here?"

"Why have they diverted the river?" Cody asked.

Faraday lifted his leg from its resting place and stood,

hopping to the other side of the room to a counter top that was covered with computer print-outs, graphs, and maps.

"Look at this," he said, sifting through the paper and pulling out a sheet that was several feet long and covered in sharp resolution by parallel lines that formed an intricate overlay of curved, irregular shapes. "This is a computer-simplified example of geotomography, which is a way of taking pictures of underground geological formations in much the same way that scanners can make pictures of internal organs in the human body."

He ran his finger along a formation where the computer tracings were pushed sharply out of alignment. The interrupted formation continued for the entire length of the long paper. "This is the New Madrid Fault."

Then he indicated a point that coincided with an obvious change in the pattern of formations about midway along the length of the fault line. "Everything from here up is in the New Madrid Basin, and everything from here down is in the Patawa Preservation Area. The New Madrid Fault passes through both of them."

"There's a place upstream from here, where the whole river channel has been pushed aside and forced into an S-turn that will really give you a ride in a canoe," Cody said.

"That's right. That's where the river crosses the fault line," the geologist said.

"So?" Jill asked.

"So that's to give you a basic idea of the way everything's laid out," her father replied, sensing her impatience. "Magnum Gas has sole rights to the New Madrid Basin," he continued. "In fact, the New Madrid Basin *is* Magnum Gas.

Studies in years past indicated a potential volume of gas recovery so vast that Magnum's stock has consistently been one of the highest performers on Wall Street.

"Then about eighteen months ago, Magnum began to experience a decline in production. A few months later they hired me, principally to try to find out why."

"And why was it?" Jill asked.

"Because of the most basic of reasons. The New Madrid Basin has just about run out of gas. The older studies, done with less sophisticated methods, were simply wrong. There never was as much gas underground as Magnum had been led to believe. They should be able to continue recovering gas at the current rate for about two more years — and then that's it."

"Wow!" Cody said softly. "I bet finding that out really upset them."

"That's putting it mildly," Faraday said. "They clamped a lid of secrecy on the information, because just a rumor about something like that could cause their stock to plunge and cost their stockholders millions almost overnight.

"I did further studies, all of which supported my earlier findings, and then one day I showed my superiors something I found hypothetically interesting." Faraday moved his hand on the paper. "The Patawa Preservation Area has tremendous, massive deposits of hard anthracite coal. It's so rich with it that seams of coal actually stick out from the side of the mountains at some locations."

"Yes," Cody said. "I've seen that in several places. It's how the Patawa Indians got the coal they used. They just broke out chunks of it. They didn't have to dig for it."

Faraday nodded. "We had good geological information about the Patawa Preservation, because Magnum was interested in it a few years ago and wanted to mine it. But the state turned them down because of its status as a preservation area."

"I remember," Cody said, and he remembered well. Like Joe Tiotec, he had been horrified at the idea of huge, thundering machines strip-mining the mountains and land that the Patawas had held sacred. Fortunately, however, neither the citizens nor the legislature had been in favor of allowing such a travesty, and nothing ever came of it.

"I once did consulting work for a European company that specializes in underground coal gassification," Faraday said. "Do you know what that is?"

"I know a little about coal gassification," Cody replied. "We studied it in physics. You put enough heat to coal, and it breaks up into its by-products."

"Right," Faraday said. "Usually the coal is mined first and transported to an industrial complex, where it's heated in large retorts. But it's such an expensive process that very little coal gassification is done like that. However, in Europe and in a few places in this country, too, underground gassification is economically feasible. You start the coal burning where it is — underground. Then when it's going hot enough, you can draw off the by-products, the chief one being methane."

"Natural gas," Cody said, "Magnum's business."

"Right again," Faraday said. "And the very thing they're running out of." He returned his hand to the computer chart. "You see all these strata? They're all coal, and they run everywhere. The surrounding geological character is unique, because of the porosity and the proximity of the adjoining fault line. An underground fire started in this region could eventually produce hundreds of billions of cubic feet of methane, most of which would seep through the ground and along the fault, collecting in the vast caverns beneath the New Madrid Basin."

"Where Magnum can drill for it," Cody said.

"In most cases, they wouldn't have to drill for it. It should collect right beneath their existing well heads, and it could be there in as little as two years."

"Just when they're running out of gas!" Cody said.

"So that's what they're doing," Jill said.

Her father nodded. "Yes. I noticed they seemed unusually interested in it when I pointed out that, from a purely theoretical point of view, it looked possible. But that's all it was — theoretical. From a practical point of view, it was a disaster. Underground fires are serious matters. Out of control, they can burn for centuries. And there's no way an underground coal fire in this area could be controlled. The entire Preservation would become a hotbed. Where the coal comes through to the surface, there would be forest fires. It's likely that hundreds of square miles of virgin land would eventually be reduced to ash and ruin."

"And Magnum went ahead and is doing it anyway!" Cody said in growing alarm.

"About a month ago, some aerial infrared photographs came across my desk by mistake. I wasn't supposed to see them, and at first I hardly paid any attention to them." Faraday sifted through the stack of papers and pulled out an example. "Here's where we are right now," he said, pointing to a spot on the high-altitude photograph. "You can see the area of unexpected heat. Except for the cooler contrast of the river, all these valleys and hills should be of about the same temperature, but you can see the heat along the base of this mountain — and how it spreads through here. These pictures were taken only a few days ago. The areas of heat in the others were smaller, but when I saw them, I began to suspect what was going on."

Cody's alarm began to turn to horror. The infrared photography showed that a large portion of the land beneath this valley and the mountains at its sides was already on fire. "How can they do that? It's against the law!"

"It's against *humanity*," Jill said. In the past two days, she had observed Cody's fondness of the Patawa River and Preservation Area, and she had sympathized, easily understanding why he felt that way.

"I confronted them with what I had discovered, and they admitted it," her father continued. "They had been working on the project for nearly ten months — since shortly after I mentioned that it was possible. They flew in everything by helicopter, bringing it in at night, carrying the really heavy equipment in a piece at a time. They said they were glad I had found out about it because they needed my help. The fire wasn't spreading as quickly as they had planned, and since I was familiar with the physics involved, they wanted me to oversee the remainder of the project."

"To suggest something like that, they obviously didn't know you," Jill said, feeling a swelling of the pride with which she had always regarded her father.

He looked at her and grinned. "Thanks, honey. The fact

is they do believe every man has his price. All these men working here have theirs, and they found my price, too. After I reminded them of the horrible consequences an underground fire could have, they reminded me that I have a daughter and that she could have some pretty horrible consequences, too."

He looked at Jill again and said, "That sealed it. I tried to mollify them, saying I would consider going along with them. I played their game and talked with them a long time to find out what they wanted me to do, but I guess I didn't convince them. When I left there that night, they had someone follow me. I went one way and shook them, then doubled back to the house to get you. They knew I would be heading for the authorities, and they had to stop me, so they sent out a helicopter. You know the rest. They kept you within their reach and kept me here to spread their fire."

"I don't understand," Cody said. "If you're trying to spread a fire, why would you be diverting water underground? It seems like that would just put it out."

"If it were just a small fire, or a fire that isn't very hot, that much water *would* put it out. But this fire is big and hot — so hot that the water molecules are broken down into hydrogen and oxygen. And that actually *feeds* the fire. Those rumblings that you've heard — it's hydrogen exploding, expanding the fire. It can travel along cracks and other underground passages and cross uncombustible strata to ignite coal deposits in other areas. They've bored vent holes in several locations to aid the movement of the gas."

"We found one of them," Jill said, "a pipe with steam coming out of it."

142

"So every time you add water, the fire gets bigger," Cody said.

"Yes, but it's a delicate process. That's where they were having trouble, why they wanted my help. They weren't putting in enough water. Because the substrata are so porous, a lot of what goes down the hole actually drains away. There are fissures and cavities that have to be filled first, before the water can have any effect on the fire. But they didn't trust the sensors and instruments. They were afraid they would put in too much water, resulting in steam explosions that would break through to the surface."

"What would that do?" Jill asked.

"For one thing, it would attract a lot of attention. Even from way out here, it would be heard — probably for about three counties. And up until about a week ago, if enough water was run in, it would have put the fire out."

"What about now?" Cody asked.

Faraday shrugged. "I don't know. Over the next couple of days you could get steam explosions pretty easily, because so much of the porous stuff is saturated. There wouldn't be much run-off, and the full volume of the river would get into the fire fairly quickly, within minutes maybe. But as I said, the fire is big now — it's under most of this valley — and I don't know that anything could put it out at this point. Besides, they're not going to let in any more water. The fire is large enough now that they can leave it to itself. By the time anyone discovers it, they will have long since closed off both of the tunnels they've constructed and destroyed all evidence that they were ever here."

Cody looked at the knowledgeable geologist in stunned

disbelief. "They can't possibly think they can get away with it!"

Faraday looked at the idealistic youngster and said, "You'd be surprised at what a company the size of Magnum can get away with, especially when they stand to profit by hundreds of millions of dollars."

"But we won't let them get away with it!" Jill said angrily. "We'll go to the —" She was going to say that they would go to the authorities, but it suddenly dawned on her that there was a real problem with such an obvious, direct approach. "Daddy, what are they going to do about *us*?"

Nathan Faraday shook his head, and Jill saw the worried look in his eyes — that selfless, fatherly look that meant his daughter's welfare was ultimately his only concern. She saw also that he did not want to have to answer her question.

# 18.

CODY RAPIDLY DEVELOPED AN ADMIRATION FOR NATHAN Faraday. Meeting him explained a lot about Jill. He was the kind of man who would naturally tend to encourage his daughter to pursue and develop her independence and self-confidence, characteristics that were clearly evident in her. Jill had told Cody that her father was brilliant, and meeting him confirmed it, but what impressed Cody most was Nathan Faraday's commanding personality.

He was a prisoner, and his broken leg severely limited his mobility, but his keepers were wary and uneasy in his presence. He looked at them directly, hard, and Cody could see their composure begin to crack. The man who brought them dinner was so intimidated by Faraday that he fell all over himself in hurrying out of the room.

There were bunk cots in one corner of their quarters and a chair, where Cody volunteered to sleep, but Faraday demanded that a third cot be brought, and it came in the arms of another man, who was equally intimidated.

Riley roamed freely around the camp, which to him didn't seem like such a bad place to be for a while. One of the strange men was easily conned into rubbing his ears and, best of all, the same man brought out a tray piled high with food scraps, including a stack of chicken bones, something Cody never allowed him to have unless they were first pressure-cooked. Riley crunched into the marrow-filled bones with joy, swallowing without concern for the remote possibility that they might do him harm.

Whenever he felt like checking on Cody, Riley knew where to find him. After eating his fill — and a little more — the setter wandered over to the building where his master's scent was so prevalent and stood up with his paws below the narrow window.

The girl came first. She cooed at him lovingly and reached her hand out to rub his ears. Then Cody came. He rubbed his ears, too, a little more forcefully, the way he really liked it, and then he called him "Traitor."

Riley didn't know what that meant, but it was said in a tone of forgiveness, so he thumped his tail and didn't worry about it. After he got tired of standing with his front feet up, he went looking for the man who was so generous with the food.

After their lights were out, Cody lay on his cot feeling so exhausted he expected to sink immediately into a deep sleep, but his mind wouldn't leave him alone. He kept thinking of Joe Tiotec.

The old man's mystic intimacy with the river of his ancestors had warned him that something evil was taking place. Little did he know, Cody thought. In a way it was good that

146

Joe died when he did. If he had lived to witness the horror of the land he loved being consumed by fire, it would have broken his heart. It should break every man's heart, Cody thought, but for men dominated by greed, the destruction of the Patawa Preservation wouldn't matter at all.

Cody saw something move in the dark, and a moment later, Jill was beside him. "Are you asleep?"

He rolled up on one elbow. "No, I can't."

"Me, either. I guess I'm too tired." She sat down on the floor and leaned against the wall. They were silent for a few moments, and then she said, "Cody, I'm sorry."

"For what?"

"For getting you into this — this mess. I really did it to you, didn't I? I mean I just snatched you up out of your life and put you smack down in the middle of some insane happening. I had no right, Cody."

"Forget it," he said. "Think of it as fate. It had to be this way. I *had* to know that this was going on. I wouldn't have it any other way. Besides," he added with conviction he didn't feel, "everything will work out all right. It *has* to."

Her voice brightened. "Listen, Cody. If it does — if somehow everything does work out all right, I'm going to try to get my father to stay in the area. I — I think I'd like to go to a regular high school, you know. From what you say, Center Ridge sounds pretty good to me. Do you think I'd do okay there?"

"Huh? Of course you'd do okay there. You'd do *great* there." Then he added in a tone of caution, "But it's not the liveliest place in the world, you know. You can get pretty bored there, too."

"I think boredom is more a state of mind than a geographic location," she said.

Cody agreed with that. It sounded like a good philosophical outlook, he told her, but he didn't tell her anything else, because he suddenly began to lose track of what she was talking about, and then sleep came over him as if someone had thrown a switch, wiping him out.

When he awoke, he thought it was a continuation of the last moment he remembered, but she wasn't sitting beside him now, and when he looked at the glow of his watch face, he realized that several hours had passed.

The building's air conditioner hummed nearby, wafting wonderfully cool air over him, and the cot was surely the most comfortable thing he had slept on in the past couple of nights, but he felt disturbed. It was a strange feeling, a restlessness, as if there was something he needed to do. For a moment he thought he must have awakened from a dream that was still affecting him even though he couldn't remember it, and then he detected a faint lightness at the window. He looked at his watch again. It was too early for sunrise. Also, the color of the light seemed somehow wrong for dawn.

Going to the window and looking out, Cody saw a now-familiar sight. Its particles effervescing from an unseen source, the mysterious cloud of light was forming near the base of the opposite bluff. As Cody had seen it do before, the light grew quickly and began to roll in on itself, wavering, pulsing. Then it began to move.

On an unfaltering, direct course, the light advanced across the narrow valley. It kept a few feet above the low line of saplings and brush that had been bent and washed flat by the force of the water, and it came swiftly toward the row of metal buildings.

It came rolling toward the portables like a thick, glowing fog, its mixture of light particles dappled with colors that oscillated to the beat of microseconds. It rolled onward and enveloped the buildings. Every window began to glow with it, and Cody thought he could feel it, heavy on him, thick in his breath.

A moment later, he felt an odd sense of warmth, as if he were beginning to glow with his own body heat. And there was something else, too — another sensation, unidentifiable yet more strangely out of place than even a feeling of intense warmth inside an air-conditioned building.

Then the cloud began to withdraw, pulling back, its nebulous mass elongating in slow release of the building.

Cody hurried to the side of Nathan Faraday's cot and shook him. "Dr. Faraday! Dr. Faraday!"

Instantly the geologist was up and alert. "What is it?"

"Look at this! Quick!"

Faraday hopped to the window and looked out. The light had already receded to near its original position on the far side of the bluff and was hovering there, a wavering sphere. Then it began to shrink and dim. A few seconds later it winked out.

"It's the same light we saw right before we found your car," Cody said. "It came all the way over here and covered up this whole building. What is it?"

Faraday nodded thoughtfully. "I couldn't say for certain, not after only a glimpse, but if I had to make a guess, I'd say it's probably methane gas. Under certain conditions, methane

149

can become ionized and give off energy in the form of visible light. Sometimes methane comes up like that out of swamps, and whenever it does, a rash of UFO sightings usually follows. One thing's for sure, though. There's enough heat and complicated chemical reactions going on beneath this valley to do all kinds of funny things. And there's no doubt that methane is venting in large quantities wherever it can find a route to the surface."

"If it was methane, how could it come all the way over here and then go back?" Cody asked.

"Again, it would just be a guess," Faraday replied, "but the ground beneath here is porous and becoming more so as it moves and cracks, yielding to the heat. The gas could have followed a fissure and seeped up from the substrata. In fact, it could still be venting, but we're not seeing it because only the initial release was ionized, and what's coming up now isn't. In any case, I'm sure there's a logical explanation. There usually is."

That was what another scientist, Dr. Joe Tiotec, had always told him, too, Cody thought — at least until near the end, when he had seemed to hedge on it a little.

On impulse, Cody moved to the door, where there was a small window at eye level. As he looked out, he put one hand on the doorknob. The door swung open at his touch.

"Holy — Dr. Faraday!" Cody stepped out and looked at the heavy padlock. It was fastened through the shackle, but the hasp had not been closed first. He showed it to Faraday.

"Somebody had to have been half asleep to have made a mistake like that," Faraday said.

"The guy who brought us the cot — he was the last one in here, and you made him real nervous. He must have —"

"We should have checked it earlier!" Faraday interrupted. "But it's not too late. It'll still be an hour or more before anyone should be moving around out there." He turned to Cody and grasped him by the shoulders for emphasis. "I want you to take Jill and get her out of here! You know your way around these hills, and as long as she's with you, I know they won't be able to harm her, and right now that's all I care about. It doesn't matter what they do to me."

"It matters *plenty!*" Jill said from behind him. She had heard them talking and gotten up to find out what was going on.

"Get your shoes on, both of you, and get away from here — now!" Faraday ordered, and Cody went for his shoes.

But Jill argued. "I'm not going without you, Daddy! I won't leave you behind!"

Her father's voice became stern. "Your getting away is our only chance — *my* only chance, too, Jill. I can't keep up with this broken leg, but when they realize you're gone and headed for the authorities, they'll think twice about making it worse by doing anything to me."

"Or they'll *make* it worse on you!"

"Jill," he said, *"get your shoes and move your butt!"*

"Yessir," she said glumly and was ready in seconds. At the door, she hugged him more briefly than she would have liked, but he was more interested in her leaving than in hugging.

"When you get to a phone, call either the state gas commissioner or the regional office of the FBI," he said and handed Cody a flashlight he had taken from a nearby drawer. "This is the only thing in here that might be useful to you. Now go!"

Cody pulled Jill's arm and got her following him. In sharp contrast to the air conditioning, the night air was blood warm and saturated with humidity. Not wanting to risk using the flashlight, they had to move slowly down the row of buildings, feeling their way along in the dark.

They had just passed the next to last portable, when a dog inside began suddenly to whine. A moment later, they heard Riley yelp and begin scratching furiously at the door. He had caught their scent as they went by, and suddenly he realized he was about to be left behind again.

"Oh no!" Cody whispered.

"He's going to get us caught again!" Jill exclaimed, following Cody in behind the last building, where they both went flat against the outside wall.

Riley continued scratching and yelping, and then they heard his muted, impatient barks. A moment later, the door opened and a sleepy voice said, "All right, all right, then go on! Beat it!"

Riley found them immediately, nuzzling them, excited. Fed, pampered, and rested, after sleeping inside, where it was cool, he was now ready to go hunting or fooling around or whatever fun thing they had in mind. He frisked through them, doing a wagging dance of joy, but when Cody got his hands on him and whispered a very specific threat in his ear, the setter went suddenly calm. The master meant business, and from the way he said it, the master *really* meant business.

They reached the road and ran headlong into the darkness, stumbling in the ruts and keeping a hand on each other to keep from falling. Approaching the clearing where the helicopter was parked, Cody hit something solid with his thigh. The impact spun him around, and he fell in front of Jill, taking her feet out from under her and dumping them both in a body-tangled heap in the dirt.

"Neat move," Jill said after they determined no serious damage was done. "And here I've been thinking you were coordinated."

"I ran into something!" he replied, feeling for the flashlight and shaking it on when it failed to respond to the switch.

A six-wheeled all-terrain vehicle with a small trailer attached was parked at the entrance to the clearing. Cody had run into its rear tire.

"Should we take it?" Jill asked.

"It's too noisy. They'd be after us as soon as they heard it start up. If we want to keep away from them, we're better off on foot." Cody started to switch the light off, but something in the trailer caught his eye. Pulling away the plastic sheet that covered it, he cast the beam onto several boxes marked with bold letters that said, "DANGER. EXPLOSIVES. HANDLE WITH EXTREME CAUTION."

"Here, hold the light," he said, handing the flashlight to Jill and tearing open the first box.

"What are you doing?" she asked.

"Blasting gel!" he said, pulling out double handfuls of skinny plastic sacks that were filled with clearish jelly.

"Cody, we need to get going!"

153

"Detonation cord!" he announced with satisfaction. "Now where are the caps? Where are the caps?"

"Cody, what are you doing?"

He searched quickly through the boxes, looking for blasting caps and fuse but without finding either. Then, in a separate, smaller box, he opened a package of square, metallic objects with dial timers on the front and a pair of insulated wires leading into a putty-like substance on the back. "I've never seen any like this, but they've got to be detonators." He looked at one more closely, turning it over in the beam of the flashlight. "Yeah, there's no doubt about it. That's what they are!"

"Cody, what are you —"

"Turn off the light," he said, taking it from her and putting it in his hip pocket. "Now hold out your arms and take this box. I'll get the other one."

"Cody —"

"Can you carry that?"

"Yes."

Feeling in the dark, Cody pulled the plastic sheet back into position over the trailer and hoisted the box of blasting gel to his shoulder. "There's been a change of plans. When we leave here, we're taking your father with us!"

# 19.

Cody got the cowling open and swung it back out of the way. He found the recessed foot wells in the fuselage, climbed up to the maintenance platform, and shined the flashlight into the compartment that housed the twin turbines. He saw very little that resembled the cantankerous engine of his old pickup truck.

"I'm getting nervous!" came the urgent voice below him. "Hurry!"

He kept looking. He had never even seen a turbine engine before, and now he was staring at a pair of the most sophisticated ones made. But he understood their basic principles, and he knew there should be easily located points of vulnerability.

His eyes went over the intricate, complex assemblage, searching for something familiar, and then he saw it — a fuel line, with quick disconnects. Holding the flashlight under his chin, he reached in with both hands and separated the coupling, pushing the ends of the fuel line aside. But he knew

155

immediately that it was too obvious. The pilot would be able to spot the trouble at a glance and remedy it.

"Get me a stick," he said. "A little bigger around than your finger. It doesn't matter how long."

She was back in moments with the stick and handed it up to him. With the flashlight off, he could make out her figure below him now. Dawn was beginning to break.

Working quickly, he whittled the stick down to size with his pocketknife and leaned into the engine compartment again, this time holding the flashlight between his legs. He stuck the sharpened stick into one end of the separated fuel line, working it in there tightly, and then he cut it off and recoupled the quick disconnect.

Now they won't find it so easily, he thought.

Standing erect on the maintenance platform, Cody's head was level with the top of the helicopter, more than twelve feet above the ground. As the diffuse, first light of dawn filtered into the narrow valley, he could see over the dense growth of saplings and brush to his next objective — the big steel sluice gates at the head of the old river channel.

Jumping to the ground, he closed the cowling, secured it, and picked up his box of explosives. "Let's go!" he said, but Jill didn't need to be prompted. She had her box in her arms and was already moving.

Staggering with their load, they ran along the road. Jill's lungs burned from the exertion, and Cody felt as if his strained arms would break off at the shoulders before they got to the sluice gates. Riley padded along behind, staying close as his master had instructed, the threat about what would happen if he didn't still ringing in his ears.

They reached the slope at the upper end of the valley and sidestepped up it, toward the top of the tunnel and the steel catwalk that was anchored into the side of the mountain. Cody shifted his load and waited until Jill was beside him again, and then they started out on the catwalk, with the admonished Riley continuing to follow.

Cody walked slowly, looking over the rail to the mechanism below. Big hydraulic arms, like giant grasshopper legs, extended from reduction units between the hinges at the sides of the steel gates and reached outward to where the gates came together to close off the flow of water at the mouth of the tunnel.

"Where?" Jill asked.

Cody shook his head and continued walking, looking for another point of vulnerability. He went all the way out to the middle, to where they were standing in the open against the sheer side of the mountain. Then he stopped and did a fast study of the locking mechanism below.

"This is the place," he announced, putting his box down and taking Jill's from her, then handing her a thick coil of detonation cord. "Shake this out."

Using his knife, Cody punched a hole all the way through one of the little plastic bags of blasting gel, each of which was about the size of a dynamite stick, and tied one end of the detonation cord through it, the gel oozing out as he drew it tight. Kneeling, he began feeding the detonation cord through his hands and lowering the "stick" over the side of the catwalk.

Directly below them was where the two hydraulic arms and the sluice gates came together in a tight, precise fit, hold-

157

ing back all but a trickle of the water. Until the hydraulic arms were powered up, the gates were secured by a pair of servo-driven bolts that moved from one gate into reinforced slots on the opposite gate. The servomechanism was mounted on a two-foot platform attached to one gate and was shielded on its sides by sheet metal, forming a box shape that was open from above, admitting hydraulic lines and permitting service.

"That should help hold the blast against the gates," Cody said, indicating the box next to the servo and lowering the first stick of gel into it. "And everything that's holding them together is centered there."

He cut the end of the detonation cord from the coil and gave it to Jill to hold, while he punched more holes in more sticks of gel and slid them down the cord to join the first stick.

"How do you know how to do this?" she asked.

"I helped Joe clear a garden spot one summer, and we used this exact kind of stuff to blow up the stumps. Now hold the cord out of the way," he said after he had slid perhaps a dozen sticks down it into the box.

One at a time, he dropped several more sticks on top of those that were threaded onto the cord. Then he began to drop them in by the handful, a half dozen or more at a time. The box was positioned directly below the edge of the catwalk and was easy to hit. Jill pushed two sticks over the edge of the catwalk with her foot, and they landed dead center in the target.

When the last stick fell to its mark, the box that contained the servomechanism, its hydraulic lines, one of the bolts, and the lever that controlled the other bolt, was packed with more than sixty pounds of explosives. Cody hoped it was overkill.

"This cord explodes, too," he explained, taking the end of it from her again and reaching for one of the three detonators he had stuffed into the pocket of his shirt. "You set it off, and in turn it sets off anything attached to it. It's how you connect two or more charges and get them to go off at the same time. But the only detonators I've ever used are blasting caps and fuses. I'm not sure about these."

He looked more carefully at the unfamiliar object. On one side was a twist dial, like that on a kitchen timer, marked off in increments of one to twenty minutes. He turned it over. The two little wires came out from under a piece of tape and went into a putty-like substance that Cody surmised was a plastic explosive. On each side of the putty was a clamp. Cody placed the detonation cord across the two clamps and pushed it down. It fit perfectly, pressing tightly against the putty between them.

"It looks like that's how it goes together, doesn't it?" he said, and Jill nodded in agreement.

"Then I suppose all we do is set the timer." He looked down the old river channel, in the direction they would be going. "How does ten minutes sound to you?"

"Whatever," she said. "Just *do* it!"

Cody twisted the dial to ten minutes, looked at it, put it to his ear. He could hear the clockwork beginning the slow process of unwinding.

Reaching down from the catwalk, he carefully lowered the detonator and dropped it with the detonator cord falling around it into the box on the sluice gate.

"How about this for good measure?" Jill asked, handing him the remaining, unused cord.

Cody dropped that in on top of everything else and stood up. He and Jill looked at each other for a split second and then they ran, Riley scooting on ahead of them lest they knock him from the catwalk.

Following the high-water mark of pushed-over and drowned vegetation, they hurried down-channel, stopping sixty to seventy yards away and taking cover behind the trunk of a sweetgum tree.

"When that thing goes, they're gonna come hauling up the road," Cody said. "We'll follow the water down to the camp and get your father. If he's right about the steam explosions being heard for three counties, then that's it as far as this little Magnum Gas project is concerned, and these guys should know that the only thing left for them to do is get out of here."

"Except that the helicopter isn't going anywhere until you show them what you did to disable it," Jill said.

"Which means that nobody leaves here, unless they take your father and us with them."

They looked at each other again, communicating in a silent way that was rapidly becoming familiar. There was uncertain logic in what they hypothesized would happen and how these men who were actively engaged in committing a serious crime would react to it, but the only alternative had been to run, essentially to do nothing, and that had become unacceptable. They shrugged simultaneously. They would see.

"Two minutes," Cody said, looking at his watch.

They crouched, watching the sluice gates, their eyes going repeatedly to the box, anticipating. Cody wondered if they were a safe distance away. The explosion was going to scatter steel like shrapnel.

"One minute," Cody said, and a few moments later, "Anytime!"

They tensed. Their jaws clamped. But instead of an explosion, a whine suddenly began nearby and behind them.

"The helicopter!" Jill exclaimed.

The whine rose gradually, the turbines gaining speed, winding up, and then suddenly they shut off, the whine dying.

"They got a fuel light," Cody said with satisfaction, "and in just a second they're going to get a bigger surprise!"

Jill saw the movement through the trees. The outer few feet of the main rotor made a lazy pass through an open space as it lost the momentum of its brief surge of power. She got up and headed in that direction, having to go only twenty feet or so before she was able to see beyond the saplings and brush into the clearing.

Two men — the pilot and the guy with the gun on his hip — were getting out of the helicopter. They walked around to the side of the fuselage, opened the cowling, and climbed up to the maintenance platform as Cody had done. Jill saw them begin to look around inside the engine compartment, and then she turned and hurried back to where Cody sat staring at his watch, his expression of anticipation having dropped to one of worry.

"What is it? Why hasn't it gone off?" she asked.

He shook his head and got out one of the two detonators

remaining in his pocket. He turned it over and looked at it again, peeling away the piece of tape that covered the ends of the two wires and exposing two tiny holes that had been concealed by one end of the strip of tape.

"Oh no!" he groaned, showing the discovery to Jill. "I should have known better. I kept thinking it was too easy, that something else needed to be done. It's a safety. The tape has to be torn off and the wires plugged into the holes!"

Jill looked at the detonator. "You mean that other one's not gonna —"

"That's right! It's not gonna do anything!"

"What about the ones you have there? Could we take one of them back?"

Cody thought a moment, remembering that they had tossed the coil of detonation cord into the box, too. "The detonator is supposed to be in close contact with the detonation cord, but if I just set it and drop it down in there on top of everything, there should be a good chance that it'll do the job. It's the only chance we've got, if we're going through with this."

They looked at each other again, and Cody said, "Wait here. Keep Riley with you. I'll be right back." He took a step, and the next step would have been the start of a sprint back to the top of the sluice gates, but at the last instant something flashed through his mind and he stopped suddenly.

"Who was at the helicopter?" he asked.

"The big jerk with the gun, and the pilot."

"What were they doing?"

"Looking at the engine."

"Where I was?"

162

"Uh-huh."

Cody groaned again, as dismally as before. "I really blew it," he said. "From the top of the helicopter, they'll be able to see me as soon as I've gone fifty feet from where we are right now, and they'll be able to stop me before I even make it to the catwalk!"

"Then what are we going to do?"

Cody's mind raced, prodded by desperation, and suddenly he began to reel in the thread of a far-out idea. "They probably don't know that we're missing yet, do they?"

Jill shrugged. "Probably not. Those two guys back there at the helicopter didn't impress me as if they were going out to look for us."

"So they wouldn't think anything special about seeing Riley, would they?"

"Well, he's been wandering around everywhere anyway. What are you getting at?"

Cody flipped the detonator over in his hands again. He plugged in the two little wires. They fit snugly, erasing any remaining doubts. Then, synchronizing his watch, he set the timer for twelve minutes.

"Riley, *ready-up*."

It was a transformation, magical and instantaneous. One moment the red setter was lying at the base of the tree, barely participating in being there, and the next moment he had snapped to attention and alertness. He moved to a position in front of Cody and snapped again, sitting. Ready-up meant *business*.

"Ready-up," Cody said, and Riley quivered with ready-upness.

"Take it," Cody said, and Riley took it, closing his mouth over it.

It wasn't what Riley expected. In these instructional exercises to which some subliminal instinct caused him to dedicate himself with a compulsion to do right, he usually received a pleasant object in his mouth, something soft and agreeable, his favorite being an old, deflated, well-chewed, leather football. This thing was different.

It felt funny in his mouth, and it tasted metallic and bitter. Moreover, it was doing something. He could sense it in his teeth and on his tongue. It was doing something funny. Before he could drop it, however, his master backed up the command with an authoritative "Hold it, Riley!" and Riley held it, keeping just enough pressure on it to secure it in his mouth without having to be friendly with it.

Cody extended his hand over his head and brought it down, pointing straight away. Riley turned and began heading obediently in that direction, not hurrying but not going as slowly as he was capable of, either. He looked back, and Cody repeated the hand signal, prompting him to move at least a little faster.

"I don't believe I'm seeing the same dog as earlier," Jill said, a little amazed by Riley's new attitude. "Do you really think he'll —"

"I don't know," Cody replied. "You saw how he was kind of slow back there when I had him fetch the firewood, and this is going to be a lot harder than that was." He shook his head. "I haven't done anything this complicated with him for a while. Go watch those guys at the helicopter. Let me know if they get suspicious."

By the time Jill returned to where she could see the heli-copter, Riley was already well into the open, trotting at a businesslike pace through the grasses and weeds at the side of the channel. Each time he looked back, Cody waved again, and he continued on.

The big man spotted him immediately, pointing him out to the pilot, both of whom were standing on the helicopter's maintenance platform. Jill saw them looking over the fuse-lage, curious, the big man becoming suspicious. A few mo-ments later, however, he laughed and they both shook their heads and returned to poking around inside the engine com-partment.

Hurrying back to tell him not to worry about the men seeing Riley, Jill found Cody standing with his hands at his sides, uttering silent threats through clenched teeth, shaking his head and groaning — all at the same time. A hundred and fifty feet away, almost at the point where Cody planned to turn him, Riley stood knee-deep in a grassy pool of water. The dorsal fin of a stranded fish stirred through the weeds in the pool, and Riley watched, his attention fixed on the move-ment, waiting for the moment to pounce.

"Oh no!" Jill said. "What did he do with the detonator?"

"Oh, he put that down before he went after the fish," Cody said.

# 20.

A<small>T ONE TIME</small> R<small>ILEY HAD BEEN REALLY GOOD AT THESE</small> hand-signal exercises, and the desire to be good at them was still there. But he just hadn't practiced them much lately, and so he was a little less sharp than he would have been otherwise. Also, the unfamiliar thing in his mouth was distracting.

At first he had been concerned that it was going to do something to him, bite his tongue maybe, or his lips. He had grabbed a rat once, and the rat had bitten him on the lip, and he had never forgotten it. The thing in his mouth made him think about the rat with part of his mind, and only the part of his mind that was left was paying attention to the hand signals his master was giving him. With his concentration split, it was a simple matter to forget everything else when he walked by the pool and saw the fish, which is what he did. He forgot everything else *instantly*.

The fish came closer, and Riley went after him, lunging

with open jaws. He hit the fish with his teeth and felt him quiver, but the fish got away, and a second bite into the cloudy water brought up a mouthful of weeds.

"He's doing it to us again!" Cody said. "He's going to get us caught. When that thing goes off, we will have had it! Not only will we not get your father out of here, but we're going to end up back there with him!"

"I've been meaning to tell you, Cody. That's some dog you have there! *Do* something!"

Cody kicked at the ground with the heel of his shoe and dislodged several rocks. He picked one up and started to throw it, but Jill stopped him.

"What if they see it?"

"Unless you have a better idea, we'll just have to take that chance."

"What if you hit him?"

"Yeah, I might do that!" Cody said and threw the rock.

When the rock came in, Riley was still trying to find the fish again. The rock splashed several feet away, but it got his attention, and he knew immediately what it was. He had once rooted a mole out of old man McAtee's flower garden, and ever since then the old guy would throw rocks at him whenever he caught the setter in his yard. When the next rock came sailing in, almost hitting him, Riley noted its trajectory and looked to see who was throwing at him.

When he saw that it was his master, he was surprised, and then he noticed something else. His master was mad. He could read his master's body language. He was so mad he was rigid.

"I'd like to break his neck right now!" Cody said, clasping and reclasping his hands above his head, demanding with the signal to "pick it up."

Pick it up? Riley looked again, alert. He would be glad to pick up the fish, just as soon as he found it. But now another rock came sailing in, and it hit so close it made him flinch and jump back.

"Pick it up! Pick it up! Pick it up!" came the signal, and Riley could see all the anger in the movement of the arms and hands. The signal changed and ordered him to move to his right. He did it, obeying, going all the way out of the water and not stopping until his master's hands told him to stop.

Cody clasped his hands together and muttered, "Pick it up, Riley! Pick it up!"

Riley looked for something to pick up, and almost immediately he caught the scent of the funny thing his master had placed in his mouth. He picked it up, carefully, still a little leery of the way it tasted and distrustful of whatever it was doing.

"He's got it! He's got it!" Jill said.

Cody turned Riley away again and got him moving toward the slope.

"How much time?" she asked.

Cody glanced at his watch. "About three minutes."

"My gosh! What if it goes off in his mouth?"

"It'll blow his head off," Cody replied and signaled him to continue up the slope.

Riley was paying attention now, and when Cody signaled him to turn to his right, he turned to his right. But within a few steps, he had to make a choice. He could either go out on the catwalk or angle off the slope, which was still in the same direction and would therefore seem permissible. He chose to angle off the slope.

"No! No!" Cody said, signaling him to go back, when he saw that he had missed the catwalk.

Obediently, Riley did what he was told. He went back. But when he was sent to his right again, he did the same thing — went past the end of the catwalk.

Cody groaned and turned him around again.

"Try sending him higher," Jill suggested.

Cody signaled Riley out, turning him up the slope. Then he stopped him when he was a few feet higher than the catwalk.

"Now try it," Jill said.

Cody signaled him to his right. Riley approached the end of the catwalk and hesitated. To go past it as he had done before, he would have to walk deliberately around the end of it. It was easier to walk out on it, so he did.

"Good boy, Riley! Good boy!" Jill said softly.

"Keep going!" Cody said, repeating the signal.

Riley continued out on the catwalk. Since he had been there already, it didn't seem like such a big deal. The steel was smooth and cool and felt good to his feet. He kept walking and looking toward his master, and suddenly Cody's hand shot up in the "stop-and-sit" position.

Riley stopped, turned, facing them, and sat.

"What do you think?" Cody asked.

"He's right above it. It looks perfect to me! How much time?"

"About thirty seconds," Cody replied, raising both arms above his head and opening wide both hands.

Riley saw the "put-it-down command," and he was happy to obey. He bent his head forward a little and dropped the thing from his mouth, the way he always dropped things from his mouth when he was told. The detonator fell to the catwalk and lay there two inches from the edge.

"It didn't fall off!" Jill exclaimed.

"Pick it up, Riley!" Cody said, clasping his hands together, and Riley picked it up. "Now put it down!" he said, throwing his hands open wide.

Riley leaned his head forward and dropped it from his mouth again. The detonator landed at the edge of the catwalk and lay there again.

"Tell him to push it off!" Jill said.

"I don't have a signal for push-it-off!" Cody said. "Pick it up, Riley! Pick it up!"

Riley picked it up on command, and then the signal to put it down came again, immediately afterwards. He was beginning to think he was doing something wrong. Maybe he wasn't supposed to put it down. He hesitated, shifting his position a little.

"Put it down, Riley! Put it down!" Cody said, throwing his hands open repeatedly. Less than fifteen seconds remained, and suddenly all he could think about was his dog's life. "Put it down, Riley!"

*"Put it down, Riley!"* Jill said, whispering it.

Riley craned his neck forward and dropped the detonator from his mouth. This time it hit the catwalk at the very edge and bounced, dribbling over the side. It fell straight down, landing right on top of the roll of detonation cord, which was right on top of the dozens and dozens of sticks of blasting gel.

"Come on!" Cody said, waving his hand frantically in the motion that meant for Riley to return at a flat-out run.

Riley trotted to the end of the catwalk, then turned down the slope and broke into an easy lope. All the underbrush and grass made fast running difficult.

"Hurry!" Cody said, moving his arm urgently. "Hurry, you crazy hound!"

Jill caught her breath in a sudden gasp behind Cody, and at first he thought it was because she was afraid Riley wasn't going to get clear in time. Then, peripherally, Cody caught a flash of movement, and he whirled around.

The big man faced them from less than ten feet away, the revolver steady and menacing in his hand, his eyes narrowed and cold. "What are you doing?" he demanded. "How did you get out of the —"

The explosion eclipsed what he was saying, and for a long instant it eclipsed everything else, too.

The gel went off with a force that Cody had not anticipated. It annihilated steel and rock, and its shock wave, amplified and directed at them by the side of the mountain behind it, was so sharp and harsh that it hurt when it popped through them. It knocked the three of them to the ground and punched out their senses.

Cody's first returning sensation was of numbness, and then his ears began to ring, followed by a gradual resetting of the circuits in his head.

The explosion had blown one of the steel gates completely off its hinges, and the other gate hung by only a few pieces of twisted metal that gave way as they watched.

Water came from the tunnel as if someone had opened a high-pressure tap but on an enormous scale. Blasting out from the side of the mountain, the river flooded into the old channel at many times the rate of the day before, and judging by its muddy color, Cody realized there must have been heavy rains and flashflooding upstream during the night.

Rolling over, he and Jill exchanged glances, reassuring each that the other was okay, and then Riley was on top of them, whining, looking for protection from whatever it was that had almost gotten him.

Behind them, the big man was getting slowly to his feet, the revolver held loosely in one hand at his side. Standing, he looked in disbelief at the huge volume of water erupting from the side of the mountain.

Cody came up and uncoiled. With all the speed he had, he drove straight for the man.

The big man tried to get the gun up and move aside, but his reactions were dulled by the explosion, and he was too slow. Cody's head rammed into the man's ribs in a blow that exploded the air from his lungs and sent the gun flying into the underbrush. Paralyzed by the spasms of his diaphragm and fighting for breath, the man clutched his side and went down in a heap.

"Let's go!" Cody shouted, rolling to his feet.

Running, they headed in the same direction as the water, which was well ahead of them and continuing in such volume that it was rapidly climbing the banks of the narrow old channel. In less than a minute, they heard one ATV and then another start up, the noisy engines rapidly accelerating.

"They're going down the road to see what happened!" Cody said.

Jill caught his arm and slowed him. "Cody! Look at what's happening to the river!"

Ahead of them, the river was beginning to back up, spilling over the low banks and spreading out through the higher underbrush and trees. It forced them closer to the road, and they saw an ATV with two men in it rocket by at full throttle.

The water continued to rise, continued to spread out. By the time they reached the camp, they were wading and Riley was half swimming in muddy water that had flooded the road and was up to the level of the portable buildings.

Supported by crutches, Nathan Faraday was standing on the wooden stoop outside the entrance to the building where they had been confined, his attention focused on a huge, turbulent whirlpool that had formed against the side of the bluff in the main channel.

The current was raging and violent. The shaft that funneled water to the underground fire was unable to gulp the tremendous volume of water fast enough, and the excess was spilling over into the rest of the valley, flooding the narrow channel beyond.

Jill saw no one else in the camp, only her father. "Daddy!"

He turned in their direction, and as they started toward him, they heard the deep rumbling begin and felt the tremors beneath their feet. For a moment, there was a ragged shaking, and then the earth was steady again.

"You've got to get out of here!" Faraday said, his voice urgent. "The fire can't take this much water!"

Cody looked at him hopefully. "Will it put it out?"

"It might, but before it does, it's going to do a lot of other things first!"

The rumbling came again, shaking the ground. A clay shelf dislodged from the side of the opposite bluff, and they watched in awe as tons of earth carrying two trees with it fell a hundred feet into the swirling water.

"And that's just the beginning!" Faraday said. "When the steam explosions begin, you're really going to see something! Now go! Don't wait for me! I'll only slow you down on these crutches!"

"Not this time, Daddy," Jill said.

"Look!" he said, hobbling painfully into the water on his crutches. "I'll do the best I can to save my own life, but don't waste yours trying to help me. You don't understand what's happening. It's too much water too fast! And that fire down there is hot — really hot — and big. This whole valley is going to blow sky high, and it's going to do it within minutes!"

Jill took in what her father said and fought back her panic. She looked around, searching for something to help get him out of here, but Cody was already ahead of her.

A steel drum that had contained fuel for the diesel generator was drifting lazily in the deepening flood water nearby. Cody went after it and brought it back.

"Okay, Dr. Faraday," he said, "we're going to help you on this, and then Jill and I are going to walk on each side to keep it from rolling over. I think we can keep you on it." He looked at the geologist and grinned. "But if you do happen to fall into the water, we'll pick you back up."

The humorous remark within these life-and-death circumstances caught Faraday by surprise. Jill saw her father react to it, at first with a kind of disbelief and then with an obvious admiration for the cool-headedness of the person who said it. His objections stopped abruptly. He committed himself to accepting their help, and Jill had a recurrence of a now-familiar thought — that of all the things she had done recently, the one thing she had done right was when she had virtually kidnapped Cody at the Kennethville Airport.

They got her father astraddle the drum, and he was able to hold his leg up enough to keep his cast out of the water.

"Put one hand on each of our shoulders, Dr. Faraday," Cody said. "That should help you stay upright. Now, let's go."

With her father between them, Jill and Cody began the evacuation. The drum was clumsy and wanted to roll, requiring nearly as much attention to keep it upright as to push it along. In addition, the water was still rising, and by the time they reached the low spot at the beginning of the road, it was waist deep. The only thing in their favor was that the backed-up water had little current.

They felt the rumble again, ragged and stronger, the tremors causing the surface of the water to shake. It died out, but only for an instant, and then it resumed, increasing. The earth seemed to be churning inside, as if it had swallowed something it could not digest. And then the incredible began.

The tunnel that was funneling water into the underground

erupted. Like a gigantic shotgun, it blasted out hundreds of tons of water, steam, and rock. The explosion blew a crater-sized hole out of the water that covered the tunnel's mouth and peppered the face of the opposite bluff with boulders weighing as much as a ton each. Then the flood water came together again, racing, pouring back down the tunnel.

"Holy —" Cody said, awed by the enormous force of what he had seen.

"And that's still only the beginning!" Faraday said.

They increased their efforts, hurrying, pushing the barrel through the water as fast as they could, following Riley, who had suddenly decided that far in the lead was the place that suited him best.

"Did everyone else leave the camp?" Cody asked.

"As soon as they saw how much water was coming in, they knew what was going to happen. There were only five of them, and none was of a mind to hang around," Faraday said.

"Or to see that you got out!" Jill said angrily.

"It was a matter of convenience," Faraday said, grimacing in pain as he lifted his broken leg higher on the barrel. "As you can see. And none of them is exactly the heroic kind. I keep expecting to see the helicopter lift off. I wonder what's holding them up."

"They're waiting for us," Cody said.

"Cody disabled the copter. It isn't going anywhere until he fixes it."

Faraday shook his head. "It looks as if you two thought of everything!"

The tunnel went off again, belching out more rock and steam, and this time there was an accompanying explosion.

The ground at the base of the bluff about fifty yards beyond the tunnel blew apart. The concussion caused a large section of the bluff directly above to shear off and fall, meeting other chunks of the earth that were still shooting skyward. Almost immediately, another explosion rent open the middle of the channel, and more rock and water, this time laden with ash, arched out over the valley.

"No," Cody said. "We didn't think of this. I didn't know it would be like a volcano going off!"

"It depends on the amount of water," Faraday said. "Who could have guessed there would be this much water in the river today?"

A look passed between Cody and Jill that meant they had taken note of still another odd circumstance over which nothing but luck seemed to have had any control, and then debris — mainly mud and water — began to rain out of the sky.

It fell, soaking them, plastering down their hair and streaking their faces and arms with dark, sooty mud. The ground bucked from the shock of two more explosions, each as powerful as the previous ones, and then a series of explosions began, advancing up-channel, rupturing open the earth and swallowing ever-greater volumes of water.

A dark cloud of noxious gasses and soot-laden steam spread overhead, growing, blotting out the growing light of early morning. The heavier crud continued to rain from it, foul and stinking, sticking to them, matting in their hair, burning their eyes.

But by now they had mastered propelling the barrel between them and were moving it efficiently. Cody was anticipating the confrontation with the other men and the pilot of the helicopter, when he heard the distant sound of the ATVs. A moment later he saw all three of the six-wheeled vehicles. They were fleeing up the side of the mountain, racing for the crest and safety of the other side.

Cody and Jill maneuvered the barrel with her father on it into the clearing. The helicopter sat in water up to its belly, its engine cowling open. Unable to discover what was wrong with it, the men had abandoned the copter and fled for their lives.

Cody had a sick, sinking feeling. Without someone to fly them out of here, they were done for.

# 21.

Explosion after erupting explosion continued to rip open the valley floor, hurling the innards of the earth into the sky, filling it with dark, suffocating death.

"This ground right here is going to go up, too!" Faraday said. "At any moment!"

No sooner had the words left his mouth, than another series of explosions began, advancing up the channel toward them. They blasted more craters in the valley floor and followed a large vein of burning subterranean coal all the way into the base of the bluff, where a deeper explosion caused another massive portion of the bluff's face to shear away.

Water rushed immediately into the newly created holes and poured underground, reloading for another series of explosions. The sky became several degrees darker with gas and steam, and a new, heavier downpour of the filthy, smelly glop began.

"I can get him into the pilot's seat by myself," Jill said, shouting to make herself heard over the din of water and

179

steam and falling debris in a world gone crazy. "You fix the helicopter!"

"You can fly this? You can fly us out of here, Dr. Faraday?" Cody said, his feeling of desperation suddenly reaching for a thread of hope.

"I told you, he can fly anything!" Jill shouted.

"But what about your leg?"

"Jill can operate the pedals," Faraday replied.

"Hurry!" Jill said.

Cody finished helping maneuver the barrel to the door on the pilot's side, then stepped up to the maintenance platform. The thick muck had already plastered nearly everything inside the engine compartment, but he didn't have time to consider if it was bad enough to cause a problem.

With shaking hands, he reached for the quick disconnect on the fuel line and parted it. He tried to remove the plug with his fingers, failed, and lost precious seconds before deciding to go for his knife. But still the wooden plug thwarted his efforts, and finally he had to resort to digging it out, removing it in pieces and splinters.

The concussion from the next explosion bent the treetops and rocked the helicopter, and the debris that fell from the sky was suddenly warmer. Cody snapped the fuel line together and jumped down. As he closed the cowling, the turbines began whining to life, and the rotor blades overhead began their arc of acceleration.

Jill had the side door open, waiting for him. He climbed in beside her, then reached down for Riley, who was paddling in the water below the door. The setter whined with joy when he saw Cody's hand reaching for him. He was in such fear of being left behind in this horrible place that he didn't mind at all being hauled up and pulled inside by the skin on his back.

"Put this on," Jill said, handing Cody a radio headset and then pointing to a jump seat behind the copilot's seat. "Sit there."

Cody sat and held Riley between his legs, pointing a finger at him and telling him not even to think about moving. Turning, Cody watched Nathan Faraday's left hand on the collective control, smoothly twisting the throttle, bringing the turbines up to speed. By the time Jill was settled in the copilot's seat, the engines were screaming and the blades overhead were blurs of steel.

Faraday looked at his daughter, and Jill nodded. He eased back on the collective, and the big helicopter lifted its skids out of the water, then immediately began to turn.

"Right pedal!" Faraday said, and Jill made the correction. The helicopter made another uncoordinated movement, and then she got the feel for it and held it steady.

Faraday brought the collective on back, and Jill adjusted for the added torque. The helicopter began a steep, full-power climb, reaching for enough altitude to clear the tops of the mountains. As Jill turned them on their vertical axis, searching for the best route out of there, Cody glimpsed the ground below.

The valley floor had turned into a steaming, smoking cauldron. Craters filled with flood water were boiling, their surfaces bucking as gasses exploded up through them. At the crumbled base of one bluff, the open ground was glowing cherry red, and as the water rushed in, another round of explosions began. Then, in an area between the camp and the clearing from which they had just taken off, the earth erupted with new fury.

They saw it coming — the expanding debris of earth and rock and water, an explosion so thick with it that it looked like a solid, growing thing.

The helicopter was almost even with the top of the bluff, when it was enveloped and struck. The bottom of the fuselage was impacted by something large and hard, and the entire machine, including both rotors, was shotgunned by rocks and debris the size of gravel. But it was the concussion itself that its occupants felt most severely.

The shock wave rose at an angle, riding the crest of the explosion, and the big industrial helicopter was hardly more than a fly in its path. Rammed skyward, the chopper was simultaneously pitched to its side, and the morning sun with its panorama of distant, hazy mountains was visible for only one quick look before they fell back, plummeting between the faces of the bluffs and falling toward the boiling, exploding valley below.

Holding Riley tightly, Cody saw Faraday react, shoving the stick hard over to counteract the fall. The helicopter responded, stabilizing and arresting its descent less than a hundred feet above the valley.

"Left pedal," Faraday said, and they began climbing again, the two pilots concentrating to maintain visual references through the thick soup of rising smoke and steam and falling glop.

The copter clawed its way up, reaching for the slice of blue sky above, and they were nearing the top again, when the screaming whine of the turbines suddenly choked back.

The turbines caught, then choked again and began losing power rapidly.

"Right pedal!" Faraday said, decreasing the collective pitch and trying to hold altitude. Hand twisting the throttle, he tried to coax the engines to resume power, but their only response was to choke back again, losing additional rpm's and running more and more roughly.

The big helicopter started down, its turbines lending only enough power to slow its descent. Faraday stretched it out, nursing the failing engines for anything left in them, but it was a losing effort.

"We're going in," he said in simple recognition of the fact, and he began slipping the helicopter toward the treetops at one edge of the valley, where the earth had not yet become an erupting inferno.

Cody thought of the plug he had put in the fuel line. Briefly he wondered if he had failed to get it all removed and this was the result. But it could have been anything — the falling muck, debris, gasses, the explosion itself — and it was academic now anyway, because the trees were coming up to meet them.

After everything they had been through, they were all going to die, Cody thought, and the strangest thing of all was how absolutely calm he felt about it. They had all given it a good try — even Riley.

Autorotating, the helicopter glided downward, sliding in toward the base of the bluff. Then, suddenly, that ground, too, seemed to erupt. An explosion of vapor arose, swelling upward, billowing into a glittering cloud.

The feeling was a familiar one this time. As the expanding gasses reached the helicopter and were whipped into a frenzy by the rotor blades, Cody felt a sensation of warmth. The cloud swirled about them, the visibility zero. In a blind, last-ditch attempt to avert disaster, Faraday was continuing to work the throttle, when suddenly the choked and dying turbines came back to life, surging to full power.

The sudden torque from the screaming engines screwed the helicopter on its vertical axis and stood it on its chin.

"Left pedal! Left pedal!" Faraday yelled, throwing the stick over. "Hard!"

Once again, the big helicopter regained stability, righting itself at the last possible moment, less than twenty-five feet from the treetops. With a delicate touch, treating the punished machine gently, Faraday eased them upward, climbing a less hostile shaft of air near the face of the bluff.

"Right pedal," he said.

A few moments later, they were over the top of the bluffs and climbing into the clear morning sky, the helicopter responding smoothly to the throttle. Faraday turned out over the mountain and made a wide, safe circle around the valley's fringes. The ground was still erupting, but with less force than before. The river had completely flooded the valley and was rolling through it now, following an old loop back to the main channel.

"I'd say there's a real good chance that the fire will be put out completely," Faraday said.

Cody had no doubt about it. Although the valley below them had been devastated, it comprised only a very small portion of the vast Preservation Area, and in time nature would heal even these scars. From this attack by man's greed anyway, much of the Patawa Preservation was saved.

Jill turned in her seat and looked back at him. "Cody —"

By the sound of her voice over the headset and the way she looked at him, he knew that she had experienced it, too — the feeling that all was well.

Cody nodded at her, and then she nodded back, smiling.